# NATIVES IN EXILE

**DIRK HARMAN**

**ILLUSTRATED BY
CHARLES BAST**

Printed in the United States of America.
Illustrations by Charley W. Bast.
Typesetting by The TypeStudio, Santa Barbara.
Cover design by Cyndi Brooks.

Library of Congress Cataloging in Publication Data
Harman, Dirk D. 1956-
Natives in exile, and other stories
1. Indians of North America—California—Needles—Fiction.
I. Title
PZ4.H2863Nat [PS3558.A62429] 813'.54 80-17517
ISBN 0-88496-291-1 (pbk.)

CAPRA PRESS
P.O. Box 2068 / Santa Barbara, CA 93120

# CONTENTS

**W**inters often passed without one inch of recordable rain on the eastern Mojave basin, but the drought-resistant natives still flowered in early spring. First came the beavertail, hedgehog and buckthorn blossoms, followed by the rabbitbrush, fluffgrass and Mormon tea, all born again in a brief yet lovely resurrection of bright colors, spiny shapes and hard shadows. Then, like cheap billboard facades, those vivid images of springtime were swiftly erased by the sandpaper gales of April, when swirling dust devils carried off the yellow paperflower blossoms, stripped away the cholla's golden crowns, and blew white yucca petals in butterfly eddies across the vast sedimentary wasteland. They finally came to rest in myriad piles against the sides of Highway Department outbuildings, vacant cinderblock motels and abandoned service stations, where they shrivelled like ashes in the baking sunlight, weathered down to nothing and disappeared.

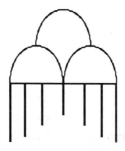

# Johnny Earth Tongue

Dry and gaunt and yellow-faced, the withered old man sat alone inside his trailer in the burning heat of August, wearing a blue denim jacket that did not quite fit. He had discovered the jacket one night earlier buried inside a trash dumpster behind a bar in Searchlight, Nevada, where he had gone to sell a rattlesnake to some biology students from Riverside. They'd paid him twenty dollars and a six-pack of beer, which he drank in the parking lot while waiting for a ride home. Before leaving, the students asked him where they might find more snakes like the one he'd sold them: olive-green and aggressive, with a highly toxic venom that attacked both the respiratory system and the nerves. The old man shrugged and told them his name was Johnny Earth Tongue.

An outdated volume of history now rested in Johnny's lap, and from time to time on that sweltering Tuesday afternoon he gazed down at the color plates inside. He could not read the captions, but was certain the illustrations portrayed the Spanish conquest of Mexico.

There was a realistic painting of four wooden caravels with cross-like masts, their decks glinting with steel lances and bronze helmets. On one page, handsome white horses with elaborate leather saddles carried the conquistadors through mountain gorges while, on another, Aztec priests danced like a frenzied flock of roosters in the bloodstained altar rooms of Tenochtitlan. He studied each picture carefully, without emotion, until he had memorized every detail. From time to time, he raised his head and squinted at the barren landscape beyond his window, judging the exact hour by the angle of canyon shadows growing across the distant face of the Big Maria Mountains.

Johnny was the oldest living human in Calizona County. While no official records existed of his birth, he often told stories describing the Mormon steamboat which became stranded on a stretch of the Colorado near present-day Solero, and he knew all about the arrival of the camel cavalry at Fort Moabi near the end of the Civil War. It was never clear if these fireside tales were firsthand accounts, or if Johnny was merely repeating versions of local history his father handed down to him in his youth, but his age was generally conceded as nearer a hundred than to ninety.

He lived alone in the snailback trailer at the northern end of the Moabi Reservation, just inside the California border. The lot was isolated, a patch of cleared gravel amidst brushy miles of hop sage and creosote. A clear view of the Big Marias could be had from the trailer's western window, while the front door opened upon a vista stretching east across the Colorado River into Arizona. Johnny spent the ovenlike afternoons of summer waiting for dusk, when his nocturnal kingdom came crawling to life. Then the aging snake shaman ventured out amont the coachwhips and zebratails with his burlap sack full of feathers, rattles and bones.

Johnny owned a car, but never drove it. He didn't know how. The rusty Ford was still hitched to the trailer, resting on cinderblocks nearly submerged in drifts of sand. Instead of driving, he daily covered miles of open ground on foot, sometimes using obscure tribal paths, other times straddling the narrow asphalt strip which ran through the reservation north towards Nevada or south back into the tiny railroad burg of Solero. Miss Mary McCloud, his sixty-year-old granddaughter, lived there. She came every other Saturday with groceries, junk mail and the illustrated history books he occasionally requested from the library in Needles. She made sure his clothes were cleaned and his hair groomed despite his apparent lack of interest. During these cursory visits he seldom spoke, and was just as content to see her drive away on the dusty track which ran past his home between town and the tribal headquarters near the ruins of Fort Moabi.

Once a month, among the piles of letters his granddaughter dutifully delivered, came a check from Washington, a federal stipend granted to all Moabi elders as a consequence of the flooding of tribal graveyards near Top Rock on the Arizona shore. A local activist lawyer named John Henry Flambeau had won the landmark decision. Johnny didn't argue over such an ironic windfall—he knew placing money in his gnarled hands would never appease the offended spirits of the old ones whose heads hung backwards—but instead used the payments to get extravagantly drunk. Much of his notoriety in Solero had to do with his tendency to buy continuous rounds in the local bars and to drink more than was healthy while appearing healthier than anyone he was drinking with. The remainder of his legend rested on his ability to handle rattlers with his bare hands.

After riding out the afternoon heat indoors, slowly turning the pages of history, Johnny looked out and witnessed a vivid sunset fluming pink and silver above the jagged range to the west. He put the book on a small table beside his cot, sipped water from a jar by the door and stepped outside. With the latest check stuffed down into the front pocket of his jacket, he set out for Solero, a seven mile hike, slightly downhill. An arid dusk burned red over the distant railyards.

Making his way along the backroad, its shoulder littered with tossed beer cans and shattered bottles, he eluded each pitfall with the reckless grace of a ceremonial dancer. His limbs were short and bony and protruded from his body like twisted stalks of arrowroot in the tumbleweed lots and tomcat alleys which he passed through at the southern edge of the reservation housing. Once away from the drab rows of cheap stucco buildings, the desert opened up around him and his pace quickened almost to a trot. A jaundiced moon hung fat and low above the dark lift of the Chocolate Mountains. Clusters of nocturnal primrose opened along the roadside. Cliff swallows arrowed back and forth, catching gnats in the last light of day, while the evening wind nudged Johnny gently on towards the bright signatures of neon flickering in rectangular grids across a tiny section of the vast desert basin.

Despite his age, Johnny remained acutely aware of his surroundings, alive and alert to his own senses the way only the best of hunters can be. He felt the hot air inside his new jacket, moving across his chest, over his slim neck, pushing the smell of sweat up into his flared nostrils. He caught the sharp scent of creosote, mingling with the softer odors of soapweed and lupine, and tasted the monsoon breeze with its flavor of approaching rain. Long before he reached the outskirts of town, he smelled the acrid smoke from diesel engines idling behind the Greyhound depot, heard the distant buzz of air conditioners fanning the bars along Main Street, and felt the deep tremor of freight cars switching off in the sooty downtown railyards.

Within an hour, he was walking the asphalt streets of Solero, where the people he greeted no longer returned the favor. Aided by his subtle gift for the invisible, he mingled for a moment with some townies sitting on the shadowy steps of the courthouse, lying to each other about dogs and birds and fish. Perfect strangers were never alarmed by his rough company, for they could not perceive the surface of his skin against the dark brick walls of the post office, they could not detect his faded clothing which blended into the lamplight like a dawn fog. Johnny continued on, heedless of the stray coyote stalking his jackrabbit shadow, undisturbed by the diamondbacks rattling under the barber shop boardwalk, ignoring the harsh warnings issued by the night ravens that watched him from drooping phonelines, for his swollen throat was an aching magnet for the clear chilled glass amid the jukebox croon of the Buffalo Nickel Saloon. That trance in which he was a permanent sojourner had lead him to a destiny of liver problems and insomnia, but it kept his spirit from walking alone.

He paused at the curb, red signals blinking DONT WALK on the pole across the street. A car pulled up beside him, its windows reflecting images of doorways and shops and a ghostlike Indian. Two shadows merged within the car and then the door flung open. A young woman's leg emerged and alighted on the curb, her body turning, her shapely figure a blue silhouette across the front seat as she leaned to kiss the driver. Johnny went by unnoticed, his eyes riveted to the glow of neon, his mouth dry in the center of his face, his dusty shoes padding softly on the pavement as the circular sign loomed larger, blinking on and off above the sidewalk: first a red Indian's head . . . BEER    ON    TAP . . . then    the    blue buffalo . . . THE BUFFALO NICKEL SALOON. He opened the paint-blistered door with a jerk and breathed the fetid barroom air smelling of smoke and sweat and stale beer odors. As soon as he reached the bar he signed over his check to the bartender and bought the house a round and within three hours sank speechless under a table between several beer-swilling war veterans who were his temporary companions. One hundred miles away, somewhere in southern Arizona, lightening forked down from black storm clouds and sent a deep shudder into the earth, the soft vibrations ringing in Johnny's ear as he lay with his head resting on the cool cement floor.

The monsoon thunder subsided at midnight as a young boy cleaned between the tables with a mop and a thick greasy man waxed the bar with a rag. The boy was thin and swarthy with cold obsidian eyes set close together in a narrow face, scanning the floor for lost change as he mopped. His search was made with such methodical precision that his boss, the burly bartender, was almost as aggravated with him as with the three customers remaining in the bar, two of them jawing at a back table with a row of empty beer mugs between them, and the old Indian somewhere out of sight.

"Come on, Ruben," he grumbled, "get the lead out of your pants and wipe this place up." He then began rubbing surreptitiously at the barstools and scowled toward the two Highway Department drunks, Bill Jackson and Danny Mendoza, who often kept him from closing early with their tiresome war stories. They did not even pretend to notice his impatience as they talked aimlessly of their uneventful military careers distorted by time and cheap whiskey into the vainglorious heroics of their youths in arms.

"And they got a snake right here in this desert," Mendoza claimed, "that will kill you fast as any of those goddam kraits of yours."

"Mojave Green?" Jackson asked.

"You bet."

"In a pig's eye!"

"I'm telling you, a kid over in Joshua Tree died inside of twenty minutes. Never even made it to a doctor."

"I seen a full-sized man go in less than five over in Okinawa. First he started to shakin' and then he vomited green water and then he was dead, faster than you could run around the block to get Doc Hazzard up out of bed."

"Geezus."

"I remember we had this nip cook, some kind of Buddhist, you know what I mean, reincarnation and all that crap, and one day he found a little snake no more than six inches long in his tent and wouldn't kill it. He kept pourin' water on it to make it go back down its hole, the dumb bastard. I guess he figured it might be his great-great-grandfather or something. Anyways, a couple of us come stumblin' in to the cook's tent lookin' for something to eat and it turns out there is a nest of yellow kraits, about twenty of them, squirming on the floor and here is this nip standing on a chair pouring teacups of water on them."

"What'd you do?"

"Hell's bells, we razed the tent with a flame thrower! Hey, Victor, bring us another beer."

The bartender looked disgusted, but he went back behind the counter and poured off two drafts. He folded the red bar rag over his forearm and brought the beers back to their table.

"This is it, boys. Gotta get home to the little woman and get me some before it's all given away."

The two men laughed.

"You might as well relax, Victor," Mendoza said, "cause when I left there was a line half way around your trailer."

"Put it on Johnny's tab," Jackson chimed in.

"Where is he?" the bartender asked.

Mendoza leaned down, lifting one leg to look under the table while his free hand reached for the cold mug of beer. He felt the warm hump of denim piled there like a sailor's duffel bag.

"Down here. Sleeping if off."

Jackson smiled wryly, "How much did he spend tonight?"

"Not enough," Victor shook his head. "He still has sixty bucks credit left on his tab. He signed his pension check over to me as soon as he got here."

"I wonder what he carries in that goddam potato sack?"

The bartender levelled his gaze on the drunks, sensing his chance to be rid of them. "You don't know?" he scoffed, "I thought everybody knew what Johnny carried with him when he came to town. No wonder you don't mind sitting by him."

"What do you mean by that?"

"Nothing."

"Well, goddamit, what has he got in the bag?"

"Why don't you see for yourself?"

"You could save us the trouble and just tell us."

"I could, sure, but what's the fun in that? I'd rather see the look on your face when you find out for yourself."

Jackson pointed an accusing finger at Mendoza. "You're the one got me mixed up with the old bastard. I told you Indians made bad drinking partners."

"Calm down, Jackson, for crissakes. You'd think it was Mojave Green he carried around in there."

Victor let out a knowing chuckle. "You said it, not me!"

The two veterans tilted their mugs and didn't stop until they were drained. Then they each got up from a table scarred with ashburns, the vinyl seats behind them punctured in places and cotton batting beginning to escape from the widest holes. Mendoza plucked some change from his pocket and left it on the table. Jackson grabbed a couple of toothpicks from a dispenser near the door and the two of them went out into the moon bright street.

The barboy worked between the tables, stopping to lift chairs onto tabletops and turning to mop where the chairs had been. Victor collected the mugs and slid the two quarters and a dime left by Mendoza onto the floor for Ruben. He worked hurriedly now, propping the CLOSED sign in the window, locking the doors, and sorting the money from the cash register into piles of tens and fives and ones, looking up now and then to observe the puppet movements of his employee. Ruben glided over the floor with his bucket-on-wheels, slopping the warm water into each corner of the room. When he was finished he rolled the mop and bucket out the back door, emptying the sudsy water into the alley. He watched the grey and white water bubble and slither away towards the grating over the storm drain at the end of the block. The lights inside dimmed, and he quickly pulled the pail upright and dragged it back through the door. Victor put the money in a canvas sack and locked it in a small safe behind the bar. He took his jacket from a post beside the cigarette machine and turned as he was about to leave.

"You can lock up tonight," he said to Ruben. "Throw the Indian out before you go."

The boy nodded, watching the rotund figure disappear into a white sedan parked across the street. When the car had revved to life and suddenly pulled away, he opened the cash register with a key hidden under the counter. He took a coin from the ringing drawer, crossed the room and placed it in the jukebox. He pushed some lighted buttons and the machine started up with a low humming of the turntable. Pools of soft purple light cascaded off the walls and ceiling around it. The music began with three long sad notes, a steel guitar moaning to a slow beat and gradually lilting higher as the other instruments picked up the tempo until the singer's voice entwined and overlapped the sound: *"When I walk along your city streets . . . and look into your eyes . . ."*

Ruben went on with his work, cleaning tabletops and lifting chairs, pulling the shades on the front door and windows, collecting stray glasses, bottles and ashtrays, dumping them in a plastic tub by the sink, the soothing music in back of each clattering noise like soft leather on a sharp wooden edge. He performed each task with a monotonous certainty, his brown face blank, gaunt, emotionless as the clock pointed towards two. He cleared the bar, took the tub to the faucet, ran the hot water, washed and rinsed and dried each glass which he lined in rows upon the shelves. Finally done, he took the trash out into the alley, came back in, set the deadbolt behind him, and after looking up to see it was a quarter past two, he sat down on a stool near the domino table and lit a cigarette. He sucked in and held the smoke a long and pensive moment. A straw cowboy hat resting at knee level below the plane of the table stirred. The slightest human exhalation moved the hat a fraction of an inch and stopped. The barboy let out a grey plume of smoke.

"Come on, Mr. Earth Tongue," he sighed, "let's get you home."

The shaman sat straight-backed in the cab of the pickup, his eyes narrowed and gleaming as he watched the bending road through dusty windshield glass. Ruben drove in silence, his own dark eyes cocked ahead towards the strip of asphalt ribbon which spun into the lamplight as they hurled forward through the desert night. Above the jagged black line of the horizon was a sky crammed with stars and constellations. A single greenish planet was going down brighter than all the rest, following the path of the missing moon. The old man saw the green light and held it in his gaze, the way a geologist might study an unusual rock fragment found in the sand.

They turned off the highway onto a dirt road. The ride became rougher, the wheels pounding hard into unseen ruts. After a few minutes of tortuous driving, they pulled up under a weak yellow lamp encircled by moths. Ruben leaned over and helped his passenger with the door. When he was standing with both feet on the ground, Johnny turned and said something to the boy in the Moabi tongue. The language was a dead one, forgotten by his children and unlearned by his grandchildren, retired to the dusty charts of ethnography, but something of its essence still lived in the words he used.

"I want to die in many colors," he chanted, "and sleep with the old ones whose heads hang backwards."

The boy nodded slowly to display his understanding, for it was in the sounds more than the words that the meaning existed. Johnny swung the cab door shut and walked up the path to his shack, listening as the heavy wheels rolled on the gravel behind him, spitting rocks and sand into the brush until the night finally fell silent and the red taillights disappeared on the road back to Solero.

When he reached the trailer door, it was already half open. He stepped inside cautiously, not wishing to disturb the nocturnal scorpions. Standing by the little iron cot which was his bed, he removed his hat and jacket, the night still warm, and in his pants and dirty undershirt lay down to sleep, his hands folded over his chest, his heart pumping under them, his forehead dry and cool. He stared at the panelled ceiling, his eyes opening and closing until they no longer saw, while he dreamt he was the snake that bit Cortez, in the peninsula of the Yucatan, where the world began.

*T*he new sign was painted on a piece of galvanized sheet metal and bolted to a wooden post along the Interstate offramp. Around it grew sparse clumps of greasewood and screwbean, with pale yellow ghost flowers poking up through thin cracks in the road shoulder. On either side of the sign stood a freshly planted fan palm. The sand was turned at the base of each young tree and the waxy fronds still gleamed in the direct sunlight, unlike the tall and dusty Washingtonias that leaned further off in the distance, down along the banks of the missing river.

At first glance, it appeared like the standard roadside welcome: chamber-of-commerce friendly and to the geographical point. The message was printed in bold white letters against an olive drab background. The four-by-eight signboard hung level to the ground, and the post had been treated with creosote. Still, something seemed wrong here. There was no town in sight, not even a motel or a gas station; just some switched-off, forgotten freight cars standing motionless on a rusty siding long overgrown with pigweed and saltbush.

From this abandoned junction you were looking at thirty empty miles across the Nevada border to Searchlight, and another fifty north to Las Vegas on Old Highway 95; it was either that or get back on the

21

*Interstate westbound with your next stop Barstow, a hundred and forty-two vacant, waterless miles away. Of course, you were probably headed somewhere else, to Laughlin or Kingman or Needles, or any of a dozen sidetrack towns in the vast horizontal drainage of the eastern Mojave basin, to Amboy or Bagdad or Essex, to Ripley, Ludlow, Earp, or Vidal, to anywhere in that wide and abandoned emptiness, to anywhere but Solero.*

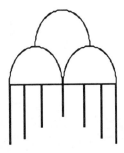

# In Search of the Elsinore Cowboy

When Emmet Ray Ford closed his gas station at sundown the little thermometer in the washroom read one hundred and two degrees. He cleaned the axle grease caked between his fingers and slid the stack of auto magazines and Western paperbacks into a broom closet behind the splintered door of the shop.

"Bath time," he said aloud to anyone, to nobody at all.

After a long, cloudless August afternoon, heat rising from the ground lay trapped beneath mountainous thunderheads boiling up over southern Nevada. Lightning streaked and flickered across the valley, fifty miles distant but headed south towards Solero. Emmet Ray locked the pumps, dimmed the fluorescent lamps in the garage, and switched off the motor under the big revolving 76 ball. Luminous yet dormant, the orange plastic sphere hung above the highway like a branded moon.

"No profit in solitude," Emmet Ray wheezed. "Looks like I took all I'm gonna take for today."

He fished a ragged wad of dollar bills from his pants, pulled the rubber band one notch tighter, and stuffed the skimpy roll away into the pocket of his blue workshirt, directly under a white namepatch with EMMET RAY stitched in red cursive lettering. His missing wife had sewn it there.

Back inside the garage office, he emptied the contents of his other pockets onto the desk: a handful of coins, mostly dimes and nickels, interspersed with pop bottlecaps, greasy lug nuts, and some unused sugar packets from Sambo's. He swept everything but his wallet and keys into a cigar box which he kept in the top drawer, behind an unopened bottle of Old Spice. After drawing the bolts on the dusty office windows, he went out back to check the restroom for snakes.

"No profit in it," he reminded himself.

A thick brass key ring dangled in his hand as he stood ready to switch out the lights for the night when he caught a glimpse of his face in the mirror above the women's sink. The combination of pale, sunken eyes and high prominent cheekbones made him the owner of a perpetual squint, like someone who had gazed too long at the last eclipse. His sharp red nose hooked down over a salt and pepper moustache, and a light beard of grey whiskers sprouted below the line of blisters that pocked his lower lip. Upon the map of his forehead, slanting diagonally from temple to brow, he possessed an impressive collection of scars. They seemed to erupt, one after another, like a tiny archipelago, growing larger and darker and more grotesque as they approached his receding hairline. Just above his head the LADIES doorsign hung, scratched and faded. He sighed again and turned off the light but remained for a time standing in the doorway, still watching the mirror, noting with peculiar satisfaction how his face lost much of its character without the scars.

After closing down the garage, Emmet Ray used his keys to retrieve a free bottle of Coke from the machine outside the shop. Then the bearded mechanic trudged across the gravel side lot, a dark blue bandanna held to the back of his neck to wipe away the grime and dust. A red tow truck was parked a few yards away from the building, under the barren limbs of an ironwood tree. Stuffing the bandanna into his back pocket, he reached into the cab and removed a coffee cup from the dashboard and a pint of Old Crow from under the driver's seat. Moving around to the front of the truck, he climbed nimbly onto the warped hood, taking his customary position for the twilight hour. He opened the whiskey first, took a quick swig, poured a shot into the coffee cup, and topped it off with a portion of cold cola. Staring out at the empty strip of asphalt and the purple hills beyond, his boot heels planted firmly upon the battered fender, he indulged himself in his nightly round of self-pity.

"No profit in working hard," he said, reaching unconsciously to test the bulge in his shirt pocket, ". . . leastwise, not enough to make any difference to you, was it, Earline?"

Earline was his wife's name, the one who had abandoned him without warning after twelve years of solid marriage. She had been gone over three months now, having skirted off with a parts salesman in early May, but the pain of her leaving had not abated. In fact, his loneliness seemed to increase in direct proportion to the rise of the washroom mercury.

Emmet Ray observed the successively darker shades of blue distancing the rocky Chemehuevi range. The near foothills rose off the desert floor only slightly darker than the sky, while the farthest peak was a bruised violet rampart arrowing up into the twilight. Beyond and to the south, the Big Maria Mountains rose ominous and black. He stared in their direction awhile, then turned his vision to nearer things. Across the road sat an abandoned trailer house, the one he had shared with Earline. The metal awnings above the door were bent down towards the ground and a fine layer of sand covered the porthole windows. For years he had survived the hot desert nights lying beside Earline in the cramped little trailer with an electric fan buzzing at his feet, reading drugstore Westerns by the stack, hypnotized with the coarse heroics of THE DOOMSDAY MARSHALL, THE RENEGADE WARRIOR, and THE TROUBLE KID, losing himself in the dogeared pages of SUNSET SAGE, riding his imagination into AMBUSH CANYON with a pair of Colt pistols in his BLAZING HANDS, wishing never again to be disturbed by the ring of a bell or honk of a horn for service. But the sandstorms of summer stampeded his daydreams, and now he spent his nights fitfully awake, listening to the canvas flap against the hollow aluminum siding of the trailer.

Sometimes he didn't even bother trying to sleep; he would drive back to town after work to play pool with his buddies at the Buffalo Nickel Saloon, or make a run across the border into Searchlight for a night of poker and beer at the Crossroads Casino. But more often than not, he remained alone at the station long after dark to drink cheap whiskey, consider his poor luck and hold long counsel with himself over matters of bad judgment with the women in his past.

"Should have stayed in San Diego after my discharge in '55," he said aloud. "You woulda liked it there, Earline. Closer to your mother and all. Summer isn't such a hell out there on the coast. No, it surely isn't."

From his seat on the hood of the tow truck, Emmet Ray could watch the entire basin falling into shadow. It lay before him like a slightly wrinkled roadmap, gradually folding in on itself towards the darkness of the river a few miles east. To the south of the swamp, on the Arizona side, the Needles were catching the last crimson wash of dusk, dark volcanic cones worn down by the eons into narrow jagged peaks, the town named after them lying at their feet. Across the valley, the evening train climbed away from Solero on the western grade, beginning the long slow climb to Barstow, then Victorville and Cajon Pass beyond. Tonight the little railroad town was nothing more than a scattered collection of signal lights blinking red, yellow and green on the sunken desert floor.

"You didn't even say good-bye!" he motioned bitterly to the first star. "Did I deserve that? Rayboy . . . your Playboy . . . Awww, Earline."

Once the sun was down, night arrived in a hurry. A pair of headlights flashed far to the north where basaltic outcroppings lined the Nevada border. They disappeared suddenly on the winding road. He stared despondently in that direction and took another drink of the whiskey from his coffee mug. When the headlights reappeared a few minutes later, he was still staring, although the mug was empty. They were much closer now. A yellowish ray beamed momentarily on the dirty windows of the trailer house. He shifted his weight forward and took hold of the the hood's lip, fighting an impulse to jump down, run to the garage, and turn on the fluorescent lamps inside. Instead, Emmet Ray remained still and held tight to his empty cup, sweat filtering through his whiskers in warm, salty drops. He didn't see a flash, but distant thunder rolled heavily through the hot night air. A coyote trotted across the road just then, not twenty yards away, nocturnal eyes shining like golden marbles as the noise of an engine sputtered from the near distance.

"Go ahead," he muttered. "Go on and pass me by."

The vehicle droned closer, backfiring once and grinding down a gear. It followed the road into a gulley and emerged just before the gas station, slowing to turn onto the packed gravel drive. The headlamps cast a pair of yellow circles against the wall of the empty building as the car angled up to the pumps. The engine idled roughly, coughed once and gave out. For a while nobody stirred inside the automobile, an older model Thunderbird. Emmet Ray shifted silently to get a better view of the car, which looked like a real classic. The first thing he noticed was the silver hood ornament reflecting the orange glow of the 76 ball within its dynamic gliding stance. He thought he could hear a strange yipping sound coming from somewhere nearby. Then the driver's side window rolled down and someone climbed through the opening, like a stuntman emerging from a spectacular wreck.

The stranger was short and skinny and wore a straw cowboy hat. He stretched his arms and legs, then spit into the gravel. The yipping sound was coming from inside the car. Emmet Ray heard the stranger curse as he lifted the hood of the T-Bird and a cloud of hot steam billowed up into his face. The smell of scorched rubber wafted through the air. His sense of business cut through the whiskey buzz and pushed Emmet Ray to action.

"Hello!" he called out.

The stranger wheeled around, startled. He peered in the direction of the tow truck, shielding his eyes as if from the glare of a spotlight, and asked, "Who's there?"

"Just me," Emmet Ray answered cheerfully, "the mechanic-on-duty. Got a problem with your car?"

"Why don't you come on out where I can see you?"

Emmet Ray dropped to the ground with a sandy crunch of his boots, balancing his mug and bottle, one in each hand. He slipped the pint of whiskey into his back pocket and approached the stranger slowly. The closer he came to the T-Bird, the more frenzied the strange yipping noise became. He moved into the orange light of the motionless globe and met the stranger's surveying stare with a nod and a smile.

"You're kinda lucky," Emmet Ray pointed out. "I was just about to close for the night."

"Looked to me like you already closed . . . and if this is luck, friend, you can have it."

The stranger stared into the overheated engine, but it was hard to know if he was smiling or scowling. His face had a dry powdery complexion, rouge markings covered his nose and cheeks, and a clown's broad grin had been painted around his mouth, surrounding what was probably a frown. Emmet Ray looked at his face in bemusement. On the dashboard, a tiny dog was barking frantically and pawing at the windshield glass as if poised to attack.

"Maybe you could use a taste of this," said Emmet Ray, pulling the pint bottle out of his back pocket.

The clown reached for the whiskey immediately. He took a deep swallow and rolled it around inside his painted mouth, shaking his head disdainfully when Emmet Ray held out the Coke to chase it. He removed his cowboy hat, which had a wooden arrow entering one side and poking out the other, and scratched the bald circle of skin on top of his pointed scalp. An orange wig was glued to the hat.

"Godawful warm hereabouts," observed the clown, still holding the whiskey. "How much further to Solero?"

Pointing due south at the meager row of blinking traffic lights, Emmet Ray burped and said, "You're lookin' at her!"

When he saw the clown tip the bottle to his lips and empty it, Emmet Ray made no objection. He leaned in against the front bumper and carefully removed the radiator cap, using his bandanna like a glove. After an initial burst of steam, the hissing gradually stopped. When he knew it was safe, Emmet Ray reached into the oily shadows under the hood and emerged with a shredded fan belt.

"There you go," said the clown."Plain old dumb luck."

"Could've been worse," Emmet Ray pointed out. "I might've gone into town already and you might've sat here all night or else burned your engine up trying to get any farther."

"Yeah," the clown agreed without enthusiasm.

"Coming from Las Vegas?" Emmet Ray wiped the grease from his hands onto his trouser legs. "They always have plenty of circus people up that way."

The clown put his hat on and the bald look went away.

"Ain't with no goddam circus," he said. "It's the rodeo. I'm on my way from the rodeo in Carson City to the one in Kingman."

Emmet Ray studied the baggy denim overalls, the battered cowboy hat, and the pointed leather boots kicking idly at the white sidewall tires of the T-bird.

"Well, how do you do, sir? A real life rodeo clown," he smiled broadly, as if this new information changed his opinion of the situation entirely. "Should have said so before, mister. I never had much use for circus people, bunch of freaks, mostly . . . but a rodeo clown is something else again. I can fix your car in no time flat. And . . . " he added, pointing at the empty whiskey bottle clutched in the clown's hand, "there's more where that came from."

The clown nodded and shrugged his shoulders, "Whatever you say, friend. This goddam vehicle has been nothin' but a misery ever since I bought it. Let me give you some advice. Never trust a Mormon. They would steal the guide dog off a blind man. I mean it. This car ran like a dream when I took it for a test drive with the salesman in Provo, the whole time he was pointing out the mountains and churches and the parks where he took his family every Sunday, the squirrel-headed sonuvabitch. So I spent my savings on it, three seasons' worth, $4995 . . . see, a clown works on contract unlike the cowboys he has to look out for, so it is possible to put a little something away for the rains. Any-goddam-way, I got about as far as the Utah line without a hitch, then all hell breaks loose. I blew a gasket outside of Ely, dropped the muffler in Winnemucca, and the driver's door jammed shut my last night in Carson City. Shitfire, even a regular-working, union-wage clown like myself can't afford that much car trouble in one month."

Emmet Ray didn't realize rodeo clowns talked so much, but he tried to be polite. He waited until he thought the clown was done with his story and then hurried off towards the garage. Somewhere in the back of the shop, in a box purchased from the same agent who stole his wife, was a fan belt which would fit the year and model of the clown's car. He retrieved his emergency fifth of Jack Daniels from behind the magazines stacked in the washroom closet, and trotted back out to the T-bird. The miniature canine yeeked ferociously at his approach.

The clown's temper improved markedly at the sight of the black label. "The good stuff," he said and quickly took it off Emmet Ray's hands and gave a generous pull on the bottle. Then he folded his long arms comfortably around it and watched Emmet Ray go to work with just the fan belt and a straight-slot screwdriver.

"What's with your dog?" asked Emmet Ray, who rarely got a chance to talk to someone while he worked.

"Oh, he gets a little ornery now and then, is all. Must be coyotes around here. They always get Geronimo's blood to boilin'."

"Geronimo?"

"Yeah, that's what name I gave him. And he's lived up to it, too. Made dogs ten times his size turn tail and run. And that's no lie!"

Emmet Ray's hands worked automatically, operating in the dark on the mechanic's keen sense of touch, a gift Earline had never fully appreciated.

"He's one of them Chee-wa-was or something?"

"Yeah, Geronimo's a pure-blood Mexican Chihuahua. Mean little bastards. When they were still wild, a long time ago, they used to travel in big packs of a hundred or more. They'd travel around Old Mexico downing steers and donkeys and such."

"Those little things?"

"Coyotes are their natural enemies."

Emmet Ray stood up and ceremoniously cleaned his hands on the bandanna, expecting some kind of compliment on his efficiency. The clown just hoisted the bottle and put a serious dent in what was left of his whiskey.

"No charge," he said as an afterthought.

"I'm obliged to you, friend," the clown's tongue was getting slower and lazier, a pattern of speech Emmet Ray was familiar with. The mechanic decided he was getting behind on the drinking, so he reached for the bottle, and proceeded to drain a good quarter of it straightaway.

"Damn," the clown shook his head, "that work sure made you thirsty."

As soon as he was finished swallowing the whiskey, Emmet Ray felt like his stomach had been set ablaze. He walked over to the cement island, steadied himself on the premium pump, and plunked down in a small puddle of grease. He could feel the oil seeping through his pants, but he didn't seem to care. The clown came over and sat down beside him. This made Emmet Ray feel a little better, since he was essentially a lonely man and, although he was not much good at conversation, he liked to hear other people talk.

The clown's voice had a soothing effect on the turmoil inside his belly. "I reckon you know Solero pretty well, huh?"

"Back of my hand," said Emmet Ray loudly.

"What part of town is the laundromat?"

"The laundromat?" Emmet Ray was momentarily confused, trying to picture a laundromat in Solero. "I don' know. I'm married and my wife takes care of my clothes." Since last April, Emmet Ray had begun lying to customers about his domestic life. The lies made him feel better about life and sometimes seemed so real that he often convinced himself they were true. He often came home after a day of talking with people he didn't know and was surprised all over again to find dinner wasn't ready and the trailer wasn't clean and Earline wasn't lying on the sofa in her underwear, watching a soap opera on television.

"Is that so? Well, I reckon I can find it. A town that size ain't got much to hide." The clown was beginning to lose his mask, drop by sweaty drop, white paste and rouge dribbling down his forehead and cheeks.

"I guess you rodeo folks can get pretty damn filthy, what with all that bull manure you flop around in."

"I'm not lookin' to wash my duds," said the clown with a trace of irritation in his voice, "There's an old bronc rider who lives in this town. A friend of mine from way back when. Runs a laundromat operation. He wrote me a letter a few months back, asked me to drop in if I was passing through."

"A rodeo cowboy living in Solero? Laundromat, you say?" Emmet Ray rubbed at his temples to try and clear the picture in his head, but it wasn't working. "I didn't know there was one. I know a few Indians who ride ditches on the reservation farmland. They got a barber shop and a hardware store and three bars, but no laundromat and no rodeo cowboys."

The clown looked at Emmet Ray in disbelief. "Mean to say you never heard of the Elsinore Cowboy?"

Rubbing his temples hadn't helped him to think, so Emmet Ray stroked his whiskers instead, trying to recall the name from one of his paperback Westerns.

"Nope," he decided after awhile, "Can't say as I have."

"I'll be damned." The clown shook his head disgustedly. Although the black paint around his lips was etched in a smile, it had begun to run at the edges. "Hard for me to believe. I got his letter not six months ago, said he retired on the Colorado River. Said he ran the only laundry operation in town. Said he was planning on doing all kinds of business on account of the new freeway bein' built through here."

"Oh, yeah?" Emmet Ray's stomach was suddenly a bag of broken glass. "I guess he didn't know that the freeway never quite made it to us." He sat up in order to relieve the pain. "I seem to remember now . . . there was a laundromat built in town a few years back. Some fellow in a wheelchair ran it all by himself. Went out of business within a year. A truck came up one day and hauled off all the washing machines. Musta been eight or nine years ago, if memory serves me. Now it sits empty, corner of Columbus and Main, next door to the old post office."

"You mean I come all this way for nothin'?" The clown's temper was beginning to flare. They were completely out of whiskey. He mopped his brow and looked, as if for the first time, at the foreign colors that stained his palm and fingers. His flushed skin was beginning to peek through the makeup.

"I sure am sorry," Emmet Ray burped twice and felt immediately better, ". . . but I guess you would have been headed this way for the Kingman rodeo, even if your cowboy friend didn't live in Solero."

"Yeah, Kingman." The clown looked distracted. "You got anything else to drink? This heat has set my throat afire."

Emmet Ray stood up carefully and staggered towards the tow truck. Inside, on the passenger's seat, was a small styrofoam ice chest and inside of that two beers floated in lukewarm water. He brought them back to the T-bird, grinning stupidly. "You're in luck!"

"I know. You already told me. This is my lucky day." The clown took one of the beers, popped the top, and slurped at the warm suds flowing over the brim. "Hot beer is about all this needs to cap off the perfect day."

Emmet Ray leaned against the T-bird and drank his, listening as Geronimo growled at him from atop the dashboard. "Tell me about this cowboy. Who is he?"

"The Elsinore Cowboy? He was just about the greatest bronc-rider of his day. That's all. I was lucky enough to be there the day he rode War Path at the stockman's show in Denver. Never seen anything to match it before or since, and friend I seen a lot of crazy cowboys and wild horses."

"I bet!" Emmet Ray was feeling dizzy, but he was trying to listen to the story the clown was telling him, since it vaguely reminded him of lying in bed next to Earline with the fan at his feet and a good paperback in his hands.

The clown breathed in, took a long swig of beer, and breathed out again. Then he began his story. "He didn't ride out of Texas or Colorado or Montana, where you might expect this kind of cowboy to come from. No, he was born right here in California, in a little town on the edge of the desert near Lake Elsinore. He was raised on a horse ranch during the worst part of the Depression. His daddy was a hard man, with a soul like flint granite, but he taught the boy everything he would ever need to know about horses by the age of twelve. His mama died when he was seventeen, just when things were startin' to get better for the family. He used to describe her as a sort of shadow that fell behind wherever his daddy stood. When she died it was like a faultline moved between them. She was their common ground, and when she left they did nothin' but battle each other. The ranch went to hell, the old man took to drinkin' and whippin' on the boy, like he was tryin' to tame a young stallion. Well, the boy couldn't be broke, and one night when his daddy was lyin' asleep on the back porch with a big ol' Colt .45 across his chest, as was his habit after a night of heavy drinkin', the kid slipped out to the barn, singled out the finest quarter horse and walked it thirty miles clear to Riverside."

"Saw a stock car race in Riverside once," Emmet Ray butted in, "with my first wife, Earline."

The clown ignored him. "He told me it was to give his daddy a chance to come after him that he walked the horse the whole thirty miles, but the old man never came. When he got to Riverside, he sold the horse and bought a ticket on the next train for Albuquerque. The following morning he borrowed a saddle, paid his entry fees and won four out of five events at the New Mexico State Fair Rodeo. Nobody'd ever done that before. I was there to see it. Me and some of the cowboys took him out that night, turned out he didn't drink. When we asked him where he was from, he told us, but we half didn't believe him. It was me thought of a name for him. 'Why, sonny, you must be the Elsinore Cowboy', I told him and everybody laughed. Had a sort of ring to it, you know?"

Emmet Ray rocked back and forth on his hams, distracted by the thought of sitting beside Earline in the racetrack grandstands. "Al Unser won it that year . . . or was it his brother, Bobby?"

The clown didn't seem to be there anymore. He was gazing sternly across the highway, past the rundown trailer house, towards the snaking black shadow of the river. The sweat crept under his makeup in chalky bubbles, giving him a cartoonish look. His entire body suggested the sad and depthless quality of a man who had lived his life to the limit, and knew there was not much left. His voice grew hushed, tonelessly falling in on itself as he spoke.

"He was just the best there was, that's all. Roped calves faster, busted meaner broncs, wrestled the biggest steers.

Entered more competitions, pulled down more winnings, Durango to Calgary, and clear into Mexico they knew his name, the one I given him. He was the champion cowboy, the one everybody knew the point scores of, since he was the one they was all aimin' to top. I was a friend, since I didn't have to compete with him. He told me things he wouldn't tell another cowboy. Not just about his family, but the things he knew about horses, the tricks he used to get the best out of an animal, spitting in a bronc's ear just before the chute opened, or pinching a dry chili pepper under a bull's nose, anything to get the best ride in the show."

"You mean he cheated?" Emmet Ray asked.

"If makin' a twelve hundred pound Brahma jump like he just sat on a hornet is cheatin', well that's what he did. As a matter of fact, it was a Brahma that finally got the best of him. I remember it like it was yesterday, musta been twenty years ago now. A little sawdust arena outside of Reno, mighta been the 4th of July, I picture lots of kids wavin' little flags. Lord, I can see it clear as anything. When his name came up on the loudspeaker everybody yelled and hooted and stomped their feet. He got that kind of reaction wherever he went in those days. Had his picture on the posters the rodeo used to advertise the event. He was at his peak right then, not that it changed him much. He was always a hard one to talk to. I guess I was about the only fella he talked to regular. Anyways, he had drawn a mud-colored brammer name of Rotten Belly, a big ugly bull with a reputation to match. The Elsinore Cowboy didn't say nothin' after the draw, that was his custom, but you could see he was pleased 'cause he wouldn't have to pull no tricks to get the kinda ride that scored points. Ol' Rotten Belly would do all the work and all he had to do was ride him. I was on the fence that day for the bull rides, Sam Lewis was workin' the dirt. I had a good view when Rotten Belly came into the chute pen. He pulled his usual stunt, tried to roll over on one of the loaders. The crowd loved it. When the Elsinore Cowboy climbed up and over and down into that pen everything got quiet. Nobody wanted to miss it when the chute sprang. He took his time cinching on, too long I thought, he usually wasn't one to fuss, but I guess Rotten Belly's reputation had somethin' to do with it. Well, finally he gave the signal he was ready and his free hand went up and the bell rang and then the chute flew off its hinges, no shit, the damn thing just jumped right off the front of the goddam pen and twirled into the dirt, right where ol' Rotten Belly planted his feet for his first buck, only his feet got tangled up between the slats of busted door and he went down like he'd been shot with a buffalo gun. The Elsinore Cowboy, who had the fastest reactions of any man I've ever known, didn't have time to get off before he was pinned under the damn bull, whose front legs were broke. It was an awful sight, man and bull and door all tangled up and turnin' circles like they was caught in a twister, and it happened so fast nobody moved before it was way too late anyway. I don't remember jumpin' down off the fence, but I remember lookin' that bull in the eyes from a distance no further than the one between you and me and not even feelin' what you could call fear. Numb was what I was. A dozen men were there beside me, but it was the longest minute of my life cuttin' him loose once somebody shot ol' Rotten Belly and we rolled the carcass off our cowboy."

"Geezus H. Christ!" After finishing his beer, Emmet Ray could feel a sickening tickle of nausea creeping up from the base of his throat. "He was dead."

"No," the clown whispered, "shoulda been, but no, he wasn't dead. In fact, he never even lost consciousness. We didn't move him until a helicopter came with two doctors from Sacramento. They flew him off the mountain down to a hospital and saved his life. I retrieved his hat from under a goddam cigarette sign and took it with me when I went to visit him the next week. He smiled when he saw it, all beat to hell like it was. They had him cast in plaster and wired up to a big machine, but he never mentioned any of it. Funny, but all he wanted to talk about was his daddy's ranch in Elsinore, how he used to get up in the mornings before anyone else to feed the pigs and chickens and milk the cow. It was the quietest time, he told me, and he started to cry, only no goddam tears would come. I just sat there like a damn idiot, course there wasn't nothin' I could do. I offered to write his daddy and tell him what had happened, but he wouldn't have it. After that, I had to go. The rodeo was in Boise and that was where I went. Later that year the Japs bombed Pearl Harbor and I went into the Army, didn't have a chance to get back to Sacramento to say good-bye. When I came back four years later, my ship came in to Oakland and I tried to track him down, but no luck. I heard some stories, tried to follow up on them, but they all washed out. One story had him doin' stunts for John Wayne pictures in Hollywood, another placed him preachin' born-again gospel on a radio station in Dallas. None of it was true. I even went by the ranch in Elsinore back around 1950. Drought had come again and wiped out everything. Nobody could remember what happened to the old man, much less where his son had ended up after runnin' off like he did. So I quit lookin'."

"Sorry to tell you this," Emmet Ray slurred, "but I never heard of any Elsinore Cowboy in these parts. Didn't he have some other name . . . like Ned or Mike or Davey?"

"I don't know."

"You don't know?" Emmet Ray asked, "What about the letter sayin' he was in Solero? Didn't he sign it?"

The clown sat melting beneath the orange light, crumpling his beer can and staring pensively into the desert, as if trying to come to an important decision. "Ain't no goddam name good enough for a man like that."

"Uh-huh," Emmet Ray grunted, pretending to understand. He was feeling the whiskey worse than ever and didn't want to think too much, but something told him the clown was a liar. It didn't really matter, but a vague uneasiness began to gnaw on the nerves at the base of his spine.

"I mean to say, the letter wasn't signed by name. Just his mark, the one he always made. I know it was him that wrote it, 'cause—" A flash of purple light and a piercing squeal cut him off in mid-sentence. The chihuahua was turning nervous circles inside the T-Bird, leaping from dash to seat and back again in a frenzy.

"What the hell?" Emmet Ray sat up, only half-alert.

The clown sprang to his feet, "Did you see that?"

Emmet Ray lurched to his feet, yelling, "No!"

"Lightning just hit that trailer across the road!"

The mechanic turned, whirled drunkenly and tripped over the curb of the pump island, falling flat on his face. When he hit the ground he didn't move. He tasted lime and gravel, and thought he could hear the approaching of horses. The ground felt comfortable enough despite the hard surface, as if a warm blanket was slowly being pulled across his body. Just before he drifted off, he heard a shuffling sound behind him, a low throaty curse, and then there was a sharp, cold pain just above his left ear, like an icicle being driven into his skull.

Emmet Ray Ford opened his eyes squinting into a pink desert dawn. He struggled to his knees, trembling from the terrible throbbing inside his left ear, and tried to brush the grit from his mouth and beard. Planting both hands forward in the gravel, he coughed up a bitter mixture of beer, whiskey and Coca-cola. Gasping deeply between heaves, he focused on the familiar shape of a black-labelled bottle in front of him, one end slightly darkened with blood.

"No profit in it . . ." he muttered between gasps, ". . . took about all . . . there is . . . to take."

The clown was gone. With him went the nervous chihuahua, the T-bird with the fancy hood ornament, and the skinny wad of dollar bills that had been in Emmet Ray's pocket the night before. The mechanic climbed to his feet and stumbled towards the garage. He burst into the shop, knocking over a wooden chair, and reached for the cigar box inside his desk. He dumped its contents onto the desktop. Grabbing a handful of change, he stepped back out into the oppressive morning sunlight and found his way to the ice machine on the shady side of the building. ALL-O-MATIC ICE declared the red letters above the coin slot and metal lever . . . UNTOUCHED BY HUMAN HANDS.

"No profit in it," he said to anyone, to nobody at all.

Emmet Ray dropped the coins into the machine one by one, then pulled on the lever. He bent to capture the round hollow chunks of ice in the folds of his dirty blue bandanna. When it was full, he walked over and sat down beneath the solitary ironwood tree with the bandana clamped behind his ear. Sitting there with his back against the spindly grey trunk, he began once again to tabulate his losses, to contemplate his scars.

*I*t had always been a town built on shifting
foundations. Even the handsome, long-boned natives
who first camped on the sandy greasewood flats to the
east of the river were annually forced to retreat to
higher ground. For untold ages the muddy Colorado,
swollen Nile of the West, overran its banks each spring
and again in late summer, depositing rich pockets of
alluvial silt which provided natural seedbeds for year-
round planting.

These were the Moabi Indians. Their ancestors
migrated from southern Mexico at about the same time
the Mayans vanished mysteriously from the verdant
jungles of the Yucatan. They wandered over the Sierra
Madres and across the Sonoran Desert, before finally
settling along the great brown river. There they
established an agrarian culture based on the cultivation
of corn, melons, and squash. The women wove reed
mats and fashioned water jugs from the dark river clays.
The men were amazing long distance runners, routinely
traveling one hundred miles a day to visit and barter
with the neighboring Chemehuevi, Yuma and Havasupai
tribes.

The Moabi tongue was musical in intonation and thick
with ancient meaning. The tribal shaman would dream
over the antics of Coyote, Beaver, Hummingbird and

*River Woman. These tales were then translated into a cycle of lyrics for the people to learn and sing at ceremonial dances. The songs explained the nature of the world, gave secret names to things and described the heroic deeds of Mastamaho the Creator. In this manner the Moabi people acquired a mythology of dreams.*

# Coyote Brings Fire to the People

Coyote Tom was looking for Mr. Willy Two Childs. He wanted someone to drive him across the Nevada border into Searchlight, and he figured that Willy was the man for the job. His own car, a purple '54 Ford Custom Deluxe, hadn't run since the night last May when Walter Bullfrog's cousin's husband poured sand into the gas tank as a way of getting even for certain indiscretions committed by Coyote and his friends at a rodeo dance over in Kingman. But now it was late August and he could feel the sharp heat of the asphalt through the wornout soles of his cowboy boots.

The Saturday morning streets of Solero lay desolate under a white-hot sun. The incessant buzzing of barroom air conditioners filled the alleys and side streets with a monotonous racket. Route 66 punched through the heart of town, past the boarded-up courthouse, post office and laundromat, then looped off towards the gray lunar hills hovering at the far western edge of town. Ground heat sweltered over the flatness of the railyards, giving the rusty collection of abandoned freight cars a submerged appearance, like an aquarium shipwreck.

Coyote Tom peered through the doors of every bar on the block—the Rainbow Room; BUD's (Beer and Wine); even the Buffalo Nickel Saloon which was normally off-limits to Indians. He crossed the parking lot outside the VFW outpost, but Willy's battered flatbed truck was nowhere to be found. After he had exhausted all the possibilities downtown, Coyote wandered into the outskirts, walking slowly through the neighborhood of neat little railroad bungalows with manicured palm trees and green squares of grass in front, then on past the trailer homes of the sunbelt pensioners with their colored gravel and cactus gardens, and finally out along the dusty back streets where squalid plywood shacks were temporarily inhabited by Mexican migrants. He had reached the Interstate frontage road and was facing a ten-mile walk home when he chanced upon Miss Mary McCloud, who was pulled off to the side of the highway with a flat tire. After allowing Coyote Tom to change it for her, she reluctantly agreed to taxi him over to the reservation center, since she was headed that way with a bag of groceries for her grandfather.

Miss Mary was a strange and secretive person who shunned close contact with anyone. She possessed a dark red tattoo in the middle of her forehead in the shape of a compass star. She took in laundry, repaired the torn clothes of railroad workers and highway construction men, and lived in quiet mystery inside the little one bedroom house her white grandfather left to her mother at his death. Rumor on the reservation had it that she was a *bruja blanca*, a halfbreed witch, but Coyote Tom didn't hold stock in those old superstitions. He knew he could take care of himself, and, besides, a ride with the devil himself seemed like a better choice than walking ten miles home under the brutal August sun.

"Your spare looks fine," he mumbled when he climbed into her big rattling Plymouth, "but I'd get that tire patched soon as you can. Roads around here tend to put holes in things."

She didn't bother to thank him, staring straight ahead as she put the car into gear and lurched out onto the northbound lane of Old Highway 95.

"Lookin' for a friend of mine," Coyote Tom mentioned. "Maybe you seen him? Mr. Willy Two Childs?"

Miss Mary gazed stonily out through the windshield dust as the Plymouth gathered speed. Coyote Tom followed her gaze beyond the highway, off to where the afternoon thunderheads were stacking up several miles to the north, like giant anvils suspended high above the desert floor. The sky overhead was an empty, searing blue.

"No," he muttered after awhile, "I guess you ain't."

They rode in silence from there. The rutted highway ran northeast through the greasewood flats that skirted the ancient river delta. About five miles out of town, the reservation road branched eastward and the Plymouth swerved onto it. The terrain gradually declined almost to sea level and the sand grew darker and loamier as they left the clusters of greasewood and creosote brush behind. Soon the barren landscape was interspersed with combed rectangular fields of black topsoil and, further on, green sections of alfalfa in various stages of growth. This was Moabi country.

Coyote Tom had been home from the war six months now. At first it was good to be back. He had taken a part-time job assembling chainsaws in the new McCullough factory over in Havasu City and had moved onto a houseboat out along the Five Mile Road in the middle of the swamp. He played cards with Willy and the boys every Tuesday and Friday night, telling stories about things he'd seen in Kaneohe, Okinawa and Phue Bai. He had taken some shrapnel from a mine explosion near the end of his tour and sometimes, if it was late and he was mixing whiskey with his beer, he would peel off his T-shirt and let them examine the network of scars on his stomach. Lately, however, he found himself feeling edgy and restless, somehow distanced from those who had always been his friends. He was getting tired of too many card games, too much beer drinking and too few women who loved without charge. Things in Solero just didn't change fast enough to suit him anymore.

Staring out across the flat *bajada*, his mind had drifted all the way to Nevada before Coyote looked up and realized that Miss Mary was driving much too fast down the straightaway farm road. He watched uneasily as the speedometer ticked past the mark at 65 . . . then 70 . . . 75 . . . 80 . . . 85 and he wondered if maybe it would have been wiser to walk, as the stone-faced seamstress stared straight ahead through the filthy, bug-splattered glass, unconcerned when the Plymouth hit 90 and began to shake right down to its vital parts. The front end was vibrating like a weight-loss machine when they tore past the stop sign at Eagle Feather Drive. They were rapidly approaching the reservation headquarters where there was always a car or two stopped in the road and children kicking balls back and forth across it. Coyote Tom didn't say anything, figuring by now there wasn't much he could tell her that she would be able to hear, much less pay attention to. The Plymouth was pushing one hundred miles per hour and ringing like an old-fashioned school bell before Miss Mary finally turned to him and spoke.

"I seen your friend, that Two Childs mister," she said.

"What?" Coyote Tom couldn't hear her above the fire-alarm clang of the engine.

"Mr. Willy Two Childs!" she shouted. "I seen him around."

"Yeah?" Coyote Tom squirmed a little as the adrenalin began to pump through his blood. A quarter mile up the road, he could see the next stop sign, one he was very familiar with, one which required a ninety-degree turn to the right or left, meaning even if she tried to negotiate it, the car would probably roll over on its side, ejecting him circus-style through the window to break his neck and die in one of his tribe's alfalfa fields. However, despite his vivid premonition, this didn't happen; at precisely the moment when the least hesitation would have provided them both with a fast and fiery death, Miss Mary removed her black leather shoe from the gas and pumped the brake pedal for all it was worth.

The Plymouth fish-tailed back and forth down the empty two-lane road. The smell of scorched rubber came up through the floorboards in a nasty stench. The car finally stopped about six feet past the stop sign at the edge of a drainage ditch full of turgid green water, facing an unseeded field covered with black fertilizer. The car's engine gave off a wispy grey smoke. Miss Mary fixed her round black eyes on Coyote Tom and did not bother to smile.

"Mr. Willy Two Childs," she said in a calm, almost hushed voice, "is a no-good, filthy, Godless drunk."

"Yes, ma'am," Coyote Tom fumbled a few seconds with the door before catching the handle and letting himself out. "Nice day. Think I'll walk the rest of the way in. Thanks again for your kindness."

His hands were shaking and the sweat on his back clammed his T-shirt tight against his skin, and the muscles had tightened up around his bowels. It was a feeling he had grown used to in Viet Nam. He was only now beginning to understand just how used to it he had finally become.

Half an hour later, Coyote Tom found Willy Two Childs'
beat-up old flatbed parked in the dirt lot behind the
American Indian Church of God, next to the reservation
drugstore and pool hall. He went looking for his buddy in
the pool hall first, but the place was empty. Being a
Saturday afternoon, this struck Coyote as highly unusual.
He pushed through the swinging screen door that
separated the drugstore from the poolroom and asked the
old woman behind the counter, Naomi Fish Dreamer,
where everyone had gone to.

"Where you been, Coyote?" she laughed. "Sleepin'
under a rock? Everybody been talkin' 'bout nothin' else all
week! Today is the day, you know, the day he come to save
us."

"Who?"

"Ain't you heard nothin' 'bout it?"

"Hell, Aunt Naomi, I gotta work for a livin'. I can't sit
around here every day like Chief Longbow and clip my
nails and listen to the daily bull session."

The toothless old woman glanced around at the
cinderblock walls, as if someone unfriendly to her cause
might be secretly listening in, then turned to Coyote and
whispered, "It's Brother Gabriel, the prophet man."

"That guy on the radio?"

"You heard 'bout him, then?"

Coyote Tom pulled a strip of beef jerky from a jar on
the counter and began to chew on it, savoring the salty
taste. Naomi's eyes narrowed behind her thick-lensed
glasses. Since he had been back from the war, she always
let him have the first piece free.

"Sure, I heard his show once or twice on the way back
from Searchlight."

"What business you got in Searchlight?"

Coyote Tom grinned then, and shook his head. "A
young man has certain needs, Aunt Naomi."

"What you need is a nice big Moabi girl, make you a wife, give you some fat little babies. My grandaughter Louise ain't seein' nobody."

"Whoa, now," Coyote laughed. "How'd we get off on your grandaughter Louise? I just want to know where my buddies are."

Naomi frowned and adjusted her glasses, then told Coyote the story. "Well, it all starts maybe two weeks ago. Some posters show up on the headquarters bulletin board and on phone poles around the reservation. Then we start hearin' 'nouncements on the radio. And yesterday a truck come down the road with these big loudspeakers strapped on back, and Brother Gabriel's voice blarin' the message that ever'body oughta come to hear him preach this afternoon down by the river. He say how we got souls just like white men do and we can't let the devil have them and he's gonna help us save ourselves from the fires of hell. You shoulda heard it, Coyote. It was really somethin'. The whole tribe gone down to the river this morning to wait for him and hear him preach in person."

"Is that right?" Coyote Tom worked the leathery meat thoughtfully between his teeth. "So they all went to the river?"

"Yep."

"Everybody?"

"Everybody gone down to hear him preach and maybe save their heathen souls."

"Not everybody, Naomi," said Coyote Tom. "Not you."

She smiled thinly, as if sharing a well-kept secret. "That just right, Coyote, not me."

"Why not?"

"'Cause I don't believe a word he say." She planted her hands firmly on the counter, ready for any objections. "All a lotta Holy Book hokum, you ask me."

"Aha," Coyote Tom smiled big in agreement. "You ain't by any chance seen Willy Two Childs in that bunch of fools that went down to the river?"

"Sure did. He the leader of them fools," she said. "He proba'ly the biggest fool in the bunch."

"Thanks, Aunt Naomi," said Coyote Tom, patting the old woman's shoulder and pinching another strip of jerky as he left.

From the drugstore he walked around the side of the church and looked into the cab of Willy's truck. As usual, the keys were hanging from the ignition. An empty whiskey bottle rested on the passenger's seat. Coyote Tom opened the driver's door and climbed in behind the wheel. The truck's engine turned over, shaking the chasis hard and blowing a grey cloud of smoke out the rusty exhaust pipe before coming to an unsteady idle. It wasn't far to the river, but the sun overhead was pounding down and Coyote Tom didn't want to get nailed on the way.

He took a rutted back road away from the reservation center, passing along the tumbleweed fringe of a lime-dusted field. After half a mile, the field ended abruptly and the dark, loamy dunes returned, signalling close proximity to the river. Several cars and pickups were parked in the dirt ahead, nosing off into the thick green rabbitbrush which grew on the banktops and hid the water from sight. Coyote Tom cut the engine and coasted the flatbed down off the packed dirt into loose alluvial sand. As the truck pitched to a halt and he climbed out of the cab, Coyote could hear someone's braying voice coming from beyond a tall curtain of yellow tules.

He followed a narrow footpath under a stand of cottonwood trees into the sedge grass along the riverside. Other voices murmured in the near distance, cut short by the shouts and cries of the ranting prophet. When he was almost upon them, Coyote turned off the worn path. He moved stealthily through the dry reeds, making his way around behind the crowd until he came to a place under a dead tamarisk where the ground was clear and he could crouch and watch the proceedings unnoticed.

Brother Gabriel was a tall skinny man in black twill pants, white dress-shirt and a red silk bowtie. His shirtsleeves were rolled up above his knobby elbows and he was standing knee-deep in the river, holding an open Bible and shouting scriptures at the tribe in a clear, booming baritone. A voice that big didn't seem to fit inside a man so skinny, but it was easy to see that he had captured the tribe's attention. They were all there: Chief Longbow and his wife; her ten brothers and their wives and children; a dozen other elders and their families; along with more people his own age than Coyote Tom could remember seeing gathered all in the same place at one time. He saw Willy Two Childs and Walter Bullfrog and Leonard Yellow-knife, hunkered down by the river's edge, rubbing elbows with the tribe elders. It didn't really surprise him to see most of the people there, spending their Saturday afternoon in pursuit of spiritual redemption. But he couldn't understand what Willy and the boys were doing there.

Until he saw the angel.

She was standing off to the side, a brown-skinned young woman clad in a white cotton dress and clutching a brass collection plate to her bosom. While the elders and their families bowed and prayed, Coyote Tom noticed that Willy and Walter and Leonard had their necks craned south towards the girl.

"Blessed is he who reads aloud the words of the prophecy, and blessed are those who hear, and who keep what is written therein; for the time is near," Brother Gabriel quoted the passage without looking into the book, "Grace to you and peace from him who is and who was and who is to come, and from the seven spirits who are before his throne, and from Jesus Christ the faithful witness, the first-born of the dead, and the ruler of kings on earth." The preacher paused to eye the crowd gravely, then went on. "To him who loves us and has freed us from our sins by his blood and made us a kingdom, priests to his God and Father, to him be glory and dominion for ever and ever. Amen."

"Amen," the elders whimpered, groveling on the muddy shore.

"Behold!" railed the preacher. "He is coming with the clouds, and every eye will see him, every one who pierced him; and all the tribes of earth will wail on account of him. Even so. Amen."

Many of the people were moaning and yessing and crowing their amens, completely wrapped up in the spell of the prophet's words. Coyote Tom smiled to himself, because his friends were also wrapped in a spell, although he could see their thoughts were not on the kingdom to come. After watching them awhile through the screen of brush, an idea began to take shape in the Coyote's head. The prophet's voice was growing more emphatic by the minute and a few faithful listeners had ventured into the brown water with him. Coyote waited awhile longer, working out his plan, then turned and retraced his steps, leaving the scene as carefully and quietly as he had arrived.

He came out beside one of the cars and looked inside. There was a balled-up T-shirt lying on the back seat. He reached through the open window and grabbed it. In another pickup bed, he found a length of rubber hose, which he carried off along with the shirt and headed back to Willy's flatbed. From there he took the empty whiskey bottle and, slipping one end of the hose into the fuel tank, syphoned off enough gas to almost fill it. He then stuffed as much of the shirt as he could into the bottle's mouth, so that some of the the gasoline was sponged up into the fabric. Finally, he grabbed some matches from the dashboard of an open Chevy and walked back towards the dead tamarisk.

By now, several Indians had been coaxed down off the bank and into the river with Brother Gabriel. They were mostly old women, along with a few of the kids, heads hung low with the accumulated weight of their guilt and shame as they waited for a chance to be redeemed. The rest of the tribe remained silent and watchful, many of them kneeling in the reddish-grey mud as they listened to the preacher. A few of the elders had joined Willy and Leonard and Walter, dividing their attentions between the preacher and the girl.

"Bretheren!" jabbered Brother Gabriel, "come beside me . . . and stand humble in God's river of love . . . great blood-colored river . . . river of Jesus blood that washes away all human sin . . . come, buhhrothers, and stand humble beside me . . . and let my hands be instruments of the Lord!" He raised his gnarled hands above his head, holding the Bible and gazing skyward, as the people crouched before him in the murky shallows. Just as he was about to reach down and touch the first one, he stopped and looked at those still waiting on the shore. "If you will not enter these healing waters, then open your purses and make sacrifice to God! My daughter, Ora, will take up the collection. Now, who will be first to stand humble in the healing waters of Jesus? Who? WHO?"

And as the women in the river clamored toward Brother Gabriel, the men on shore were stumbling over each other to be the first to drop their money into the offering plate held outstretched in Ora's slender arms. The tumult of male bodies surging forward out of the muck caused a small commotion, as some of the older and less agile became bogged down in the slippery earth, and were nearly overrun by the younger and more eager likes of Walter Bullfrog, Leonard Yellowknife, and Willy Two Childs. This created just enough distraction to provide Coyote Tom with the opportunity he had been waiting for. He struck a match and held it to the gas-soaked shirt

until it caught and then tossed the bottle high into the
skeletal limbs of the dead tamarisk, where it exploded in a
great blossoming of yellow flame.

Coyote dove away into the rabbitbrush a safe distance
from the tree. The fire spread quickly among the high,
tinder-dry branches, and the tamarisk began raining red
embers of burned-away bark. Soon a column of black
smoke was funneling up on convective air currents into
the empty waxen sky.

Down along the riverbank, things were getting messy.
Those who had been in the river, waiting their turn with
Brother Gabriel, all rushed the shore. The men struggling
over each other in the grey slime along the shoreline had
ceased moving and remained frozen in various stages of
repose, like mud wrestlers captured in a public sculpture.
Daughter Ora was turned towards the fire, so that her face
took on the same infernal quality as her hair. Brother
Gabriel, too, was staring at the blazing vision, looking
more perplexed than anyone at this apparent sign of God's
displeasure.

The fire rapidly worked itself down through the upper
stems and branches towards the hollow center of the tree,
like multiple fuses burning back to the same explosive keg
of dynamite. Under the intense pressure of the converging
heat waves, the gourdlike trunk did in fact blow to pieces
and what remained of the tamarisk crumbled instantly to
the ground. The bulk of the tree folded in on itself, cutting
off circulation to feed the flames. There was a great deal of
popping, crackling and smoking, but the fire had
essentially been extinguished almost as quickly as it began.

By that time the people coming out of the water had
entangled themselves among the less pious members of
the tribe on shore, leaving Brother Gabriel alone in the
river. He was moving slowly into deeper currents, staring
quizzically at what was now a smoldering black stump,
still holding the Bible aloft as the water came up around

his shoulders. Ora didn't seem to know what to do. She had the plate cradled under her bosom, but nobody was reaching for it anymore, the focus of the tribe's interest having shifted dramatically after the tree exploded.

Coyote Tom watched in amusement as the confusion over what had just transpired struck the crowd. Walter Bullfrog was seated in the lap of Chief Longbow's wife, Lovedia. The chief himself lay prostrate in the mud under a pile of squirming grandchildren, and several of the women had to rush to his rescue. Talking all at once, the tribe exchanged descriptions of what they had actually seen. One old woman claimed to have noticed a white dove sitting in the dead tamarisk just before the fire broke out. A teenage boy remembered killing and burying a rattlesnake under the same tree a few days earlier. Some considered it an act of God, while others feared that the devil was mischievously involved. A few clung to the rational explanation that it was a freak phenomena of nature known as spontaneous combustion. The more cynical members of the tribe asserted it was all just a trick staged by Brother Gabriel to weasel more money out of the misguided faithful. Many members of the tribe began to agree with this last interpretation and their feelings seemed to be confirmed when the prophet floated out over his head and was carried lazily downstream by the current. Finally, when the only things visible above the water were his tiny head and an outstretched arm still holding the Bible aloft, someone climbed into a nearby rowboat and went to fish him out.

Circling back away from the river unseen, Coyote Tom came out of the reeds near the line of parked cars and scrambled into Willy's truck. Easing into reverse, he backed onto the dirt road and drove away quickly. By the time his people finally began to emerge from the rabbitbrush, still arguing over what had actually taken place, Coyote was half-way to Searchlight.

*T*o-ho-poc was the Moabi word for "river-crossing." The village changed location often due to the caprices of the seasonal floodtides. For several hundred years the adaptable tribe lived undisturbed along the fluctuating waterline, until it was abruptly discovered and claimed under the royal dominion of his excellency, King Ferdinand of Spain, by Father Diego Garces in 1776.

Father Garces was on a difficult journey across unchartered territory and took full advantage of the Moabis' evident lack of suspicion or guile. His traveling biographer noted how one of the Spaniards grew disenchanted with Garces' leadership at that time and left the expedition unannounced, taking with him several horses and a small fortune in stamped gold coins. He was never seen or heard from by another white man again, but the legend of his treasure lived on in the folklore of the region. One story told that the gold was hidden somewhere in a rugged range of dead volcanos a few miles to the southeast, while another version claimed it was buried in the badlands to the west.

The rest of Garces' party dined on mesquite beans and chuckwalla stew all that summer, staying long enough to erect the first Christian monument in the region on a bluff overlooking the dry riverbed. The next spring, after the Spaniards had gone, runoff torrents undermined the bluff and the white adobe church floated away in a swirl of frothy red water.

# The Washout

The two-lane backroad connecting Searchlight to Solero was a forgotten stretch of highway known as Old 95. It ran road map straight between the two towns, descending gradually down the basalt plateau of southernmost Nevada onto hot riparian desert along the lower Colorado River. The route looked direct enough on paper, but this was just an illusion of cartography. Like a natural roller coaster, the terrain fell and rose a hundred times, crisscrossed with geological faults and folds. The road cut was beginning to erode badly in places. Highway maintenance presented numerous ongoing problems, and the neglected blacktop had acquired a reputation for detours, breakdowns and fatal wrecks.

Jose Pomona was driving Old 95 about an hour before dawn on Sunday morning. It was the last week in August and a group of monsoon thunderheads had blown in overnight from Mexico. Flashflood warnings were in effect throughout the eastern Mojave and several Sig-Alerts had been posted by the CHP. Any other night he would be home warm in bed, but, as luck would have it, this was Jose's weekend for emergency duty. The supervisor's call woke him around midnight and now he was driving back and forth from Solero to the Nevada border, inspecting the treacherous old highway, making sure it was still safe enough to keep open.

He steered the Highway Department pickup due south through a series of steep washes, rising to the barren crest above one and downrushing into the next with the ticklish pull of inertia tugging at his stomach. After a recent cloudburst, the rain had slackened to drizzle and the sky was clearing in patches of deep indigo between the black clouds. A dark belt of patched asphalt gleamed in the twin circles of light cast ahead by his brights. Jose drove with the window down, his left elbow pointed into the wind, as the cool rain-washed air filled the cab with the sharp smell of wet creosote.

Guiding the pickup with both hands firmly on the steering wheel, Jose listened to an early morning gospel program on the radio, a red thermos bottle cradled between his legs. Now and then he reached down with one hand and brought the uncapped bottle to his lips, tightening his grip on the wheel with the other hand as he drank, never letting his eyes leave the road. Jose considered himself a superior driver. In all his time with the Department, over twenty years now, he had never had an accident or received a ticket, not even an equipment violation.

The voice on the radio sermonized in a harsh low tone. The signal originated from a mysterious ghost station located somewhere out in the local desert, where an outlaw evangelist issued his weekly warnings about Armageddon and the impending doom of the civilized world. The unauthorized broadcast was a favorite among the otherwise agnostic citizens of Solero who listened to Brother Gabriel's diatribes every Sunday morning and then adjourned to the nearest barroom to argue over their personal interpretations of this week's sermon. Jose listened because he liked to hear the Bible quotations, often recognizing passages his grandmother had read to him when he was growing up in Calexico. He also liked the fervent, near-hysterical quality of the preacher's voice. Something urgent in it gave his weekly drive through the desert a quality of spiritual significance it did not otherwise possess.

". . . and Jesus went down into Galilee," the radio rasped, "and sat with his disciples by the water, saying, 'I will open my mouth in parables, I will utter what has been hidden since the foundation of the world.' Think of it, brothers and sisters. Then he left the crowds and went into a house. And his disciples came to him, saying, 'Explain to us the parable of the weeds of the field.' And he answered, 'He who sows the good seed is the Son of man; the field is the world, and the good seed means the sons of the kingdom; the weeds are the sons of the evil one, and the enemy who sowed them is the devil; the harvest is the close of the age, and the reapers are angels' . . ."

So it was that angels were on Jose's mind that early morning in late August, driving down Old 95 with both hands wrapped tight around the wheel and the open thermos cradled between his thighs, when he first noticed the odd red light glinting in the darkness up ahead. He couldn't make it out at first, but he instinctively took his foot off the gas and lightly toed the brake. The truck was halfway up a long grade, climbing out of another rocky wash. Near the top of the climb, the strange wavering light winked like a misplaced traffic signal.

When she suddenly came into the highbeams, the girl standing in the road appeared petrified, like a deer in jacklight, unable to react to her own fear. Jose hit the brakes hard and jerked the wheel to the right. The truck skidded sideways, missing the girl by no more than the length of Jose's arm. The truck pitched off the wet blacktop, fine jets of rainwater fanning out from beneath the tires. For an instant the vehicle was airborne, and the giddy weightless feeling pulled again at Jose's belly. Then the pickup rocked to earth with a loud WHOMP, bounced once, and came to a halt in soft white sand several yards beyond the road shoulder.

The truck had somehow managed to stay upright. After the wrenching takeoff and the rocky landing, Jose was amazed to find that the coffee was still steaming in its container between his legs with only a few drops spilled onto the seat. His left foot had slipped off the clutch and the engine was dead, but the ghost preacher bawled on with a mindless persistence from a speaker inside the dashboard.

". . .'Just as the weeds are gathered and burned with fire, so will it be at the close of the age' . . ."

He turned the ignition off. The absolute quiet served to calm him, although his heart still pounded at the base of his throat and his hands were twitching involuntarily on the wheel. Slowly, carefully, as if testing himself for some deep internal injury, Jose swung the door open and climbed out of the cab of the pickup. He was glad to know that all of his vital parts remained in working order, that his pants were dry, and that there was no more damage to the Department truck than some scraped hubcaps and a couple of half-buried tires. The two wheels on the passenger side were plowed up to their axles in the soft white silicate. Standing in the loose sand, his legs felt somehow extended, longer and more rubbery than normal, but other than that he felt fine. He always carried an array of shovels, picks and post-hole diggers in the truckbed, so being stuck was no big problem, maybe an hour of digging and that was all. He suddenly realized with a sense of dismay that this was his first accident. He immediately thought about the boys back at the Highway

Department, Jackson, Wynn and Mendoza, razzing him
for driving too fast in the rain. But nobody could say it had
been his fault. Angels had distracted him.

He looked back down the road towards the girl, but
couldn't see her anymore. His heart pushed harder on the
wall of his chest. Had he hit her after all? His eyes adjusted
slowly to the lack of light. Things took on thick shadowy
features in muted tones of blue and gray. Towards the east
clouds were getting some color into them, but the land
was heavy with darkness. Jose thought about his bed back
in Solero, with his blankets lying smooth and undisturbed.
Then he saw the girl, still standing in the middle of the
road, defined against the blacktop by her yellow poncho.

He took a sip of coffee from the thermos, as if this were
all routine, something that happened each Sunday
morning just before dawn on Old Highway 95. As he
watched her approach, Jose quietly considered how close
he had just come to killing this person he was about to
meet.

The girl carried something in her hands. She walked
with odd halting steps on her tiptoes, as though she were
crossing a shallow stream, holding whatever it was out in
front of her like a letter of introduction. When she got
close enough, he recognized what she clutched in her
hand. It was the rear reflector off a car. That is what had
made him brake, the red reflection of his own headlamps
in that plastic-coated mirror. She must have been standing
in the road awhile. Her hair plastered against her skull,
giving her a thin, emaciated appearance. Jose noticed she
was shivering hard. He quickly retrieved a wool blanket
from behind the seat of the truck, and walked up to drape
it over her shoulders. She flinched when he held out the
blanket, then pulled the canvas poncho off over her head
and wrapped the grey blanket tightly around her
shoulders.

He judged her to be maybe fifteen or sixteen. She was wearing a yellow rainslicker, blue jeans, and white tennis shoes. Her hair, a streaked blonde color that looked to be dyed, was tied up in a ponytail and hung off the back of her head like a question mark. Her face was thin, almost gaunt. The bones of her cheeks seemed to be pinching the skin around her eyes, so that she stared ahead with a wide-awake expression. When she got close enough for him to hear, she stopped abruptly and spoke in a loud, exaggerated voice.

"The man is . . . down," she sobbed, trying to catch her breath. "The man is . . . down."

"What?" asked Jose, looking around to see if anyone else had been involved in the accident. "What's the matter now?"

"The man is down, I tell you . . . Hurry!"

"What man? I can't see anyone else here."

"You don't know who he is, but he's down. Over there. We have to help him, just hurry, please."

"Hold on, little sister. What are you tryin' to say?"

The girl was standing before him with the broken reflector clutched in her grip, talking in confused circles. She had a stunned look in her eyes, as if she was holding her breath underwater, staring up at him while she drowned.

"Hurry!" she breathed out. "We have to help him!"

He realized that she was looking past him, in the same direction he had been driving before the crash. The road ran uphill for another fifty yards before it peaked and disappeared into the next gulley, one more in a long series of blind washes between Searchlight and Solero. From where he was standing, Jose could tell nothing about the condition of the road ahead, but something in the girl's expression urged him to find out.

The odor of creosote was even stronger now, an oily cutting smell. The only sound he could hear as he trotted uphill was the rubbery sucking of his workboots on the wet asphalt. When he reached the top of the dunelike ridge he saw the sky opening wide distances between the clouds and he knew the rain had quit for good. It was still dark, but a purple thread was rimming the eastern horizon and he could see stands of yucca all around him in the bruised morning light.

Then he looked down and saw the washout. The worn road had finally buckled under a brief but intense flood that must have flashed riverward during the worst part of the thunderstorm. At first it appeared as a wide black gash in the highway, but, as he walked closer, a V-shaped cut in the roadbank revealed the bare subsoil six feet deep. The gap was about twenty yards across and contained chunks of crumbled highway, along with an uprooted smoke tree, the gnarled remains of several dead yucca plants, and a newer model Cadillac. The Caddy was nosed into the near bank and the passenger door was flung open. The vehicle rested at a thirty-degree angle to the sand beneath it. The rear wheels were three or four feet off the ground, hanging motionless in midair, while the front third of the car was planted firmly into the earth. Whoever had driven the car into the washout was still seated behind the wheel.

Jose approached the Cadillac with a vague trepidation. He always expected the worst in these situations. In his many years with the Department, he had seen dozens of accidents, enough not to feel too queasy about one more. Still, his pulse began to quicken and a thick bilious juice streamed into his mouth, burning his throat as he swallowed. He studied the wrecked landscape—the tongue of wet sand undermining the highway, the intricate root system of the upturned smoke tree, even the red and white factory paint job which made the trunk end of the Caddy stand out of the barren landscape like a gawdy signal flag—but his eyes always shifted focus back through the cracked windshield to the limp figure whose forehead was pressed up against it from within.

He came to the very edge of the washout, standing back a step or two from the loose footing of the overhanging asphalt, and looked down. The sun would not rise for another thirty minutes, but the sky had already lightened enough that he could now see pieces of Old 95 strewn downstream across the gulley, along with flattened columns of cactus, wind-tumbled chinchweed and various flashflood debris. The hollow shaft of a dead yucca had been driven like a spear into the bank opposite the Cadillac, almost touching the up-turned left tailfin, and creating a thin counterpoint to the hulking automobile wreck.

"Coupe DeVille," said Jose, shaking his head in wistful admiration. "V-8 with overdrive."

Then his sense of duty returned. He scrambled down the newly-formed embankment and reached the embedded hood of the car. He considered for a moment the impact it must have taken to implant such a large vehicle that deep into the sand. From his perch on the shiny part of the hood, Jose could see that the driver was a man in his mid-thirties, bearded, with long stringy brown hair. He was wearing denim overalls and a white T-shirt. He didn't seem to be conscious, but peering down into the front seat through the cracked windshield, Jose could see that the driver was breathing regularly and was not bleeding or otherwise visibly disfigured. Here was nobody's angel.

He jumped off the hood, slipping once on the loose gravel, and came up to the driver's door. He tried it, but the hinges had been jammed in the crash. He walked carefully around the car to the passenger's side. The door was propped open and one of the seat belts trailed out of the car, almost touching the sand. The seats were covered with  protective plastic. Another thing he noticed, but didn't understand until later, was that the rear windshield was marred by large half-erased numerals written in soap. As the sky began to pinken along the eastern ridge of the wash, Jose leaned in for a better look at the driver.

Whoever he was, he was still alive. Through the white T-shirt, Jose could see his rib cage expand and contract with a paced rhythmic motion. There was no blood coming from his nose or mouth, no bones broken in his arms or legs. Apparently, he had been knocked unconscious when his head hit the steering wheel. Gently, Jose took him by the shoulder and propped him up in his plastic-covered seat. This was difficult, due to the downward tilt of the Caddy. He squeezed into the passenger's seat and braced himself with one boot up against the glove box. When he was pulled upright, the driver let out a gurgle of saliva and began to cough. He struggled to catch his breath and finally, after belching twice, opened his eyes.

"Wha . . ." he gasped, ". . . the hell, where'm I?"

"Hello," said Jose. "You're here. With me. Jose Pomona."

"Are you . . . the devil?"

"I'm with the Highway Department. Are you hurting anywhere? You wrecked your car. Too bad, cause it was a beauty."

The disoriented driver looked out through the spider web of smashed windshield glass. "Where is Amy?" he asked thickly.

"Is that her name?" Jose said. "She's alright, just wet and cold is all. She saved my butt from driving into this sinkhole. Saved yours, too, I guess, 'cause I woulda landed smack on top of you, no doubt."

The driver's eyes shut for a moment, then reopened upon Jose. "Satan!" he cried. "Get back, you Lucifer, back away from me!"

Jose almost laughed. "Calm down, mister. I'm not anybody you know. You've had a blow to the head. You're not clear in your thinking right now."

"The devil wears many faces," said the the driver. "The devil has many names."

"Well, mine's Jose and I work for the Highway Department, which ain't exactly heaven, but it's awright if you don't mind working outdoors. And what is your name, if I you don't mind me askin'?"

The driver struggled weakly with the handle of the door. Sensing he was cut off from any easy escape, he turned to face Jose.

"Jesse," he said. "Jesse Bob Coulter, from Arkansas."

"Well, Jesse Bob, congratulations. You are lucky to be alive."

"Amy? Where's my little Amy?"

"Is she your daughter? You should be proud of her, then. She risked her life to save our butts, I have to tell you. She's up the hill, waiting by my truck."

Jesse fixed a glassy stare on Jose, as if weighing every word for the truth. He brought his pale hands up from his lap and wrapped them viselike around the steering wheel. He turned the wheel and the car settled another inch, bits of rock and sand tumbling onto the hood.

"I want Amy, my little queen," said Jesse. "Want to see her now, if you don't mind."

"Okay, okay," said Jose, attempting to appease Jesse, who was obviously off-balance. "I'll go and get her. I need to set some pylons anyway, before somebody running to Vegas plants their pickup in the trunk of your car."

Jose levered himself down from the passenger side to the ground two feet below. As he climbed quickly out of the wash, he looked back once, but Jesse Bob had not moved from behind the wheel. When he reached the crest again, the eastern sky was on fire, shot through with bright veins of blue turquoise. Thick bands of cumulus clouds piled up on the horizon, bleached pink by the approaching dawn. A solitary raven flew south, cawing over the scarred brown hills.

When he reached the Department pickup, the girl was gone. The piece of reflector which had probably saved his life was lying on the floor of the cab, but she had taken the wool blanket with her. This puzzled him, but he didn't have time to go beating the bushes right then. Working hurriedly, Jose retrieved a stack of hazard cones from a vertical pipe welded to the rear of the truckbed and scrambled back onto the road. He placed two in the center of each lane to warn oncoming cars not to pass and carried four with him to place on the opposite side of the washout. He wasn't that worried about traffic southbound on Old 95 at this time of a Sunday morning; who in their right minds would be in a hurry to reach Solero before daybreak? But someone was eventually going to try the old road north to Las Vegas and even in broad daylight the washout would swallow them up if Jose didn't place some pylons out to warn them off.

As he trudged back up the grade lugging the weighted plastic cones, he looked across the dunes at the sparse bunches of greasewood and creosote, searching for some sign of the girl. She had disappeared. He wondered why she would run off like that, knowing her father was hurt in the crash.

Jesse Bob Coulter from Arkansas was still seated at the wheel of his two-tone Coupe DeVille, gazing intently through the cracked windshield at the highway which appeared at eye level two yards in front of him. He seemed stunned yet alert, like a rabbit in a snare, trying to convince his legs it was still possible to move out from under the red vinyl dashboard.

"Amy?" he asked pleadingly.

"She's gone," said Jose. "Don't ask me where to or why, but she's not in the pickup anymore."

"Gone? What do you mean gone?"

"She ran away."

"What did you tell her? Why did she go?"

"Mister, I didn't tell her anything. She took off before I ever got back up there. She doesn't even know if you're alive or dead."

"You mean she left me here?"

Jose nodded. "She did seem a little jumpy when I first talked to her, but I thought it was on account of how close I came to running her over with the truck."

"She saved me."

"Yeah, she probably did," Jose agreed. "Now, you feeling up to getting out of this car? I can't guarantee that somebody else won't come along and pile up on top of you."

Jesse nodded, then closed his eyes and appeared to fall asleep.

Jose decided the poor guy was still dazed from his concussion. He thought it would be best to let him rest awhile longer, before trying to carry him out. He glanced into the Cadillac once more and then went on up the other side of the washout, carrying the pylons over his shoulder. He marched about a hundred yards up the highway and placed the orange hazard cones to warn northbound vehicles of the danger ahead. Looking south towards Solero, he thought he detected smoke from an approaching diesel engine. He wondered if it could be a beef truck from Blythe heading towards the casinos at Laughlin. He decided to wait and flag down the driver.

A few minutes passed in which the sky rolled back a pale blue canopy overhead. Jose was right. The eighteen-wheeler barrelled over the last crest and braked for the pylons. He could hear the air steaming across the pads.

"Whatta you got?" a cowboy-hatted trucker leaned his head out the window.

"Washout," yelled Jose over the noise of the idling diesel. "This next section of road's halfway down to the river. Got a CB unit in there?"

"Yeah," boomed the trucker. "I'll call the CHP."

"Have them get Emmet Ford to bring his wrecker. There's a Cadillac crashed into the ditch."

"Any dead bodies?" the trucker asked in a tone that might have been morbid if it wasn't so matter-of-fact.

"No, they were both lucky, if you can call it that. I better go see to the driver, though. He's still pretty woozy."

"How the hell am I supposed to turn this rig around?"

"There's a turnout for a mining road back a half-mile or so. Maybe you can pull it off there. It'll be a week or more before they get this stretch open again. Thanks in advance for making that call."

The trucker cursed and shoved the gears around until he had the truck backing up slowly. Jose turned with a wave and headed back towards the washout. He beat his shirt for cigarettes, realized that they were still in the pickup on the other side of the canyon, and cursed under his breath. He almost tripped coming down off the highway where the footing was particularly soft. He couldn't see into the Caddy from behind, due to the soap on the rear windshield. Stepping carefully, he came up alongside the driver's door and stopped short. The plastic cover was wrinkled where the driver had been slouched for so long. Jesse Bob Coulter from Arkansas, just like his daughter Amy, had disappeared.

The sun came up over ash-colored mountains, firing the last trace of departing thunderheads with a crimson outline. The close, towering spires of the Big Maria Mountains caught the first glaring rays before anything else. From there the light ran downhill to meet the white sands and spread out over the desert with a sweeping cast of gold. Purple lupine blossomed on the shaded slopes

alongside small flurries of brick-red globemallow. Grey
and white patches of asphalt dried on the highway,
snaking lazily south back towards Solero.

By the time he got the Department pickup out of the
sand and backed up onto the highway, it was after nine.
Emmet Ray Ford arrived, hungover and in a foul mood,
but willing as usual to make some easy money. He claimed
to have been robbed by a gang of circus freaks the night
before. When the CHP finally arrived, Jose had to listen to
him tell the whole ridiculous story again. The officer was
Rob Capshaw, out of Needles. He checked the plates and
radioed in the numbers. The word on the Caddy was that
it had been hot-wired off the lot of a North Las Vegas
dealership more than a week ago. Jesse was wanted in
seven Western states for everything from grand theft to
statutory rape. Amy was the teenage daughter of the
mayor of Ogden, Utah. Apparently, she met Jesse while
attending a church function in southern Idaho and ran off
with him on a whim to Nevada, where they spent an illegal
nine days and nights together. When the hotel detective
grew suspicious and started asking questions, Jesse Bob
wired the Caddy and took off, probably bound for
Mexico. He had passed a bad check in a motel outside of
Bullhead City and was apparently on the run from
authorities in Arizona. He didn't get too far, however,
before Old 95 swallowed him up. The truckdriver Jose
sent for help had found the girl walking on the Interstate
and gave her a ride into Solero, where she was now in
protective custody until her mother arrived from Utah.
Jesse Bob was still somewhere out there in the rocky
drainage of the Big Maria Mountains. A sheriff's
helicopter was flying in from Needles to find him.

While Emmet Ray rigged the winch, the CHP followed
Jesse's tracks a few hundred feet from the wreck. The
fugitive had gone down the wash, in the direction of the
river, but he had dodged in and out of several finger

canyons, leaving the officer unsure if he actually knew the river was within walking distance. When the winch-crank turned and the car moaned and creaked and finally tore from the ground with a sickening suck of metal on rock, the Cadillac emerged from the roadbank like a fossilized fish from a prehistoric sea. Capshaw scratched some illegible symbols onto his report sheet and asked Jose to sign it as first witness on the scene. A few minutes later the wrecker and the patrol car were gone.

Jose took another sip of cold coffee and sat in the cab to wait for the emergency road crew. He couldn't remember who was on the schedule to relieve him, either Jackson or Mendoza. He turned the radio's volume louder. The preacher warned of imminent disasters, of future floods, of drought and famine and plague about to waste the earth and rid forever the scourge of sin from the troubled hearts of mankind. Jose smiled to himself, scratching his chin, wondering just how he would tell this story to the boys back at the motor pool.

*A*lthough they heard disturbing stories from other tribes, the Moabis didn't see another white man until the first of the beaver trappers arrived in the late 1820's. He was a tough, ruthless Frenchman without education or refinement whose table manners and washing habits made the Indians seem civilized in comparison. His name was Jean Pierre Flambeau. He was the first outsider to breed within the tribe and he left a legacy of five sons who were neither Indian nor white, and who later grew into a dreaded band of renegades that blazed a trail of murder and mayhem unequaled in the territory. After Flambeau showed up with his brutal array of rifles, skinning knives and iron-jawed traps, it wasn't long before the region was overrun with similar unsavory types, greedy for pelts and the flesh of young women, but they left as soon as the beaver gave out from overhunting and another period of relative calm fell over the fertile desert valley.

# Miss Mary McCloud

Miss Mary McCloud was a tattooed half-breed seamstress with nine cats and an alabaster necklace to which she assigned the arbitrary value of ten thousand dollars. She kept a loaded gun in the drawer of her nightstand in the little adobe house on the outskirts of Solero where she had lived since birth. Her dreams were vivid with behatted men frustrated by the heavy-duty locks and bolts on the windows and doors of every room, who made midnight attempts to enter through the kitchen with an axe. She awoke each night and, with the huge pistol in her hand, marched through the musty corridors with a candle, listening for the telltale drop of the latch, so that she might fire away at the closed door with that antiquated six-shooter left by her white grandfather in 1923 to protect her mother from the same evil intruders of her dreams.

Since she had never used it, the sixty-year-old orphan didn't even realize that the gun was useless, that time had corroded the bullets and choked the barrel with clots of cat hair. She kept it nearby at noon when the mailman

passed. She carried it in her bag as she made the weekly
journey to see her other     grandfather, Johnny Earth
Tongue, on the Moabi reservation. She rushed to the
shelter of its calcified trigger whenever a customer would
send her husband for the bags of clothes she washed and
stitched for a living. Like a snake that had lost all its
venom and didn't know it, she hefted the weighty rod in
the candlelight of her evening vigilance against the
behatted men described to her in childhood by the
ghostly grandfather, the one who died in the famous
bordello fire near Whitman in 1929, leaving his
husbandless daughter and her fatherless child in the tiny
adobe house with only a Bible, a gun, and the worthless
string of alabaster.

She cared for the cats like fickle offspring, who
required her attention only at meal times and spent the
sunny mornings and hot afternoons asleep under the
wooden porch. At least they kept the snakes and lizards
away, while at night they dedicated themselves to the
reproduction of their species amidst the vulgar howls and
trash can clatter of all out feline warfare. She far preferred
the baked silence of noon, when nothing moved and the
sound of old paint could be heard blistering from the
doorstep posts. In the searing heat of late August, she
remained content darning the torn sweaters and shredded
stockings of her livelihood, calm with the knowledge that
the cats were at peace and the gun was an arm's length
away. At nightfall the cats gathered on the porch and
demanded their dinners of bad fish and skimpy chicken
wings that Miss Mary purchased for them from a busboy
in charge of dumping trash behind the diner on Main
Street. They ate from nine separate platters she had
placed around the house so that even the smallest kitten
would receive his share, and the tomcat battles were
postponed for the midnight alley in back of the
abandoned laundromat.

Miss Mary kept the necklace in an envelope tucked between the mattresses of her ancient feather bed (self-addressed, of course, so that in the event of some unexpected intrusion she might make it to the mailbox down the street before the behatted stranger could gain access to her yet undefiled abode). She lived in constant fear of being robbed and assaulted during the night by one of the strangers of her dreams. On special days, preordained by some interior clock of the mind, she bolted the doors and windows at midday, checked the street and neighbors' yards and the hall closet and the kitchen pantry for any sign of the fleeting shadow of a criminal who was after her precious jewelry, and, when completely assured of her impregnable solitude, Miss Mary lifted the sagging mattress and removed the yellowed envelope from its hiding place and carefully pulled the long, lustrous string of beads from between the paper folds, letting the slightest sigh of pleasure escape from her time-leathered lips. Then, at the mere tap of a cat's paw against the kitchen windowpane, she thrust the necklace back under the mattress and strode out of the bedroom, six-gun in hand, with eyes the cloudy color of smoke, scanning every inch of her empty house for the potential bridegroom in death with whom she would gladly exchange her .45 calibre vows.

Her Moabi father gave her the tattoo because he believed it would save her from the rantings of her white grandfather, a fanatical evangelist named Zachariah McCloud. Her father wasn't her mother's husband because the grandfather would not permit it. Her father never argued about it, but he did kidnap her from time to time during her youth and keep her with him on the reservation near Fort Moabi. The tattoo was shaped like a star and her father said it corresponded to her own personal light in the nighttime sky. She had not liked it very much when the drunken comrades of her father, a band of hatless Indians with names like Alfred

Sweetwater and Billy Lost Horse and John Crazy Snake, held her kicking body down while William No Clouds carved the insignia himself with a hot knife and the red dye of wild arrowroot. When Zachariah saw it he took the gun and was gone for two weeks before coming back with the announcement that her father was gone from the region for good. Not long after, he died in the tragic bordello fire which claimed the lives of seventeen other men and three women as well. Her mother never recovered from that shock of circumstances, the scandal which went up around the fiery death of a white evangelist in a miner's whorehouse in Whitman, Nevada in 1929. She never saw her father again, but after the fire her mother took her out to the reservation to meet her other grandfather, a Moabi rattlesnake shaman named Johnny Earth Tongue. From that time on, Miss Mary (that's what her new grandfather called her) visited him regularly as a way of preserving whatever it was that tied her blood to the earth.

Her mother gave her the slim string of beads on her deathbed and with that gesture left the world. Miss Mary stared with dark fascination at the necklace, hardly recognizing the labored exhalation of her mother's final breath. That evening at dusk she began practicing a ceremony which was to continue throughout her life, bolting the windows, latching the doors, locking herself into the only bedroom of her virginal house. She undressed slowly in the candlelight with a guarded sense of apprehension. When completely naked, she stood up and went to the mirror, gazing in tender examination of her unweathered body, wearing only the pearls and holding only the gun. She covered the tattoo on her forehead with her free hand, no longer seeing herself, Miss Mary McCloud, but looking instead upon some vestige of feminine purity glowing beneath the translucent skin, while moths fluttered against the window and automobile horns blared under the broken

stoplights of Main Street and all the other sounds that
would make her take aim in that direction at any other
time of the day or night were now no more than a seashell
whisper at the back of her hearing as she watched with
wonder the slow restoration of her girlhood beauty that no
man ever saw, like a palo verde tree fallen in the desert of
her youth—uncut, unburned, left to the slow and
unalterable desiccation of time—suddenly sprouting
tender green leaves and pink-throated flowers. Then she
awoke at the sound of a moth trapped inside the candle-
glass, sure that the illusory behatted rapist had finally
arrived. She dressed hurriedly and unlocked the bedroom
door, carrying the dim candle and the useless gun into the
endless night of her undying grief for a grandfather who
perished, a mother who died, and a father who never
returned.

"Who is that?" she asked aloud, heard her own voice
echo in the hallway, and instinctively aimed at the closed
kitchen door.

"You? Papa?"

She held up the candle, searching the shadowy corners
for some trace of another human being.

"Have you come back for me? After all this time? Tell
me why."

The empty house beat like a heart. The wooden floor
pulsed like the tight skin of a drum as she stalked the
solitary darkness, waving the candle, brandishing the
pistol, and gradually feeling the weight of her tattooed
planet being pulled into orbit. The kitchen door swung
open with a shout of wind. She saw the familiar stranger
standing in the doorway, smiling under his tall grey
Stetson. The candle blew out. The gun misfired twice and
fell apart in her hand. Hoarse laughter clouded her senses,
a vacuum of fear crippled her with its heartbeat inertia,
pounding the walls and stirring up the dust of her desire
until she could stand it no longer, unable to resist the
masculine pull of gravity that caught her as she fell.

*G*old was discovered in the Big Maria Mountains in 1869. A rogue miner came stumbling out of the red lava hills with a pouch full of nuggets as big as popped corn. The rush began within hours. Miners came pouring into the valley from as close as Death Valley and as far away as the Yukon. Tent camps were pitched on the lower slopes of the Big Maria's, evolving rapidly into a shanty boomtown. Soon there was a general store, a lumberyard and a whorehouse, along with half a dozen whiskey saloons. Interests in Denver and San Francisco invested heavily in the operation of several mines. Claims were filed and fought over, with the litigants doing battle in a makeshift court on the banks of the Colorado. The circuit judge refused to rule on anything until they built him a proper chamber, and so the construction of a real courthouse commenced in downtown Solero.

# Ashpram Stew

# (the perils of eating a white horse)

Ashpram was a liar and a recluse, a sad relic of an age gone by who still hunted for gold in the rugged mineral wasteland south of Top Rock. His appearances in Solero were rare and unpredictable, but whenever he arrived he always had another story about past adventures prospecting in the Big Maria Mountains. The tales often went on too long, following strange tangents and bizarre circumlocutions, so his audiences of eager listeners often disappeared before the end of the tellings.

The old miner's home was a corrugated tin shack tucked into the pocket of a dry canyon between two sheer cathedral walls. The two cliffs leaned towards each other near the top of the canyon, arching like a natural drawbridge overhead and dropping from time to unpredictable time a rain of red lava rocks. He ate whatever he could shoot or trap, usually rattlesnake or jackrabbit, cut into slices and slow-cooked in a black iron caldron together with mesquite beans and wild wormwort. His cooking was almost as famous as his stories, and those who had ventured far enough into the desert to sample his stew swore it was the best they ever tasted.

His family consisted of four mules, Matthew, Mark, Luke, and John, who were excellent listeners, if nothing else. The mules fed themselves, grazing on the patches of stinkweed and squawbush which grew in profusion around the miner's shack. These meager resources were supplemented by feed which Ashpram handed out at his pleasure, usually after a particularly strenuous day of labor. While they each possessed a character and personality peculiar to themselves, they all received equal treatment from their master. Ashpram loved them, berated them, punished them, groomed them, kicked them, cursed them, and depended on them to be constantly stronger, milder, and more patient then himself. They were his surrogate children, more durable than sheep, more intelligent than dogs, and occasionally more stubborn than a band of Arabian camels.

Today he arose before dawn and mounted a pair of wooden kegs on each sleepy-eyed disciple, then tied them in a train and led them down the trail, the five of them winding like a Chinese dragon down the narrow path which descended between jutting metamorphic crags into the steep river gorge. There before them they saw the blue shine of the Colorado, flat and serene as it cut its mammoth ribbon through the jagged Big Maria range. When they finally reached the bottom after an hour's hike, they followed the bank past blonde rows of marsh tules to a spit of white sand curling into a tiny peninsula, where the water piled clean sand to form its own cup of beach from the torrential vacuum of the river.

Ashpram removed the kegs and filled them with fresh water to be used for the next week's cooking, washing and drinking. While he was there he checked his trotlines, finding a bloated carp caught two days ago, foul-smelling and inedible. No catfish. He tested and rebaited the line with the visceral parts of whatever creature he had stewed that week, then carried the line out into the deceptively strong currents of the cold flowing river. The mules down the beach nuzzled the tufts of bunchgrass that grew on the riverbank, resting their round unblinking eyes on their master's strange, splashing efforts in the water. Deep guttural curses flew from Ashpram's mouth as he clambered back to shore, his ragged pants soaking wet. They did not take long to dry in the arid morning breeze, however. With the day still new, he lifted the first heavy cask and taunted the mules back to work.

"Hup, now, Matthew . . . you ugly sinner . . . hold still, I say, or I'll feed your gizzards to the carp!" One by one the four reluctant drays were loaded down, the rough miner's hands cinching the straps tight under their gorged bellies. The hoarse voice berated them, and, when the casks were finally all secure, the mellow voice coaxed them, "Good fellow, John . . . steady as a rock, you are . . . Hup!" as slowly, steadily they traversed the rising plateau that narrowed into a familiar winding canyon, the five of them, man and mules, trudging back to the origins of their trek, the mine.

The shack was built into the cliff and, therefore, had no backdoor, but the crooked doorway faced the yawning mouth of the mine and he could sit at his table while eating stew and look out upon the piled heap of tailings excavated over many years to open the deep and mysterious rupture in the earth. The corrugated tin roof protected a cot, a wooden box full of pans and kettles and lids, moth-eaten Army blankets, scraps of old magazines and newspapers, doorknobs, gascaps, corroded forks and spoons, a table and chairs made of dynamite crates, two kerosene lanterns, an antique mirror whose image was marred by bubbles of silver nitrate, iron hobbles for the mules, coils of frayed rope, battered picks and splintered shovels, a black kettle hung with wire over a pit of coals, and—displayed upon a shelf above the single unglassed window—a collection of bleached skulls, their graveyard grins clogged with brown clay and cobwebs. He had found them one by one in his haphazard diggings and now they rested undisturbed within the thin walls of his cluttered abode.

Returning with the water, he loosened the leather straps and removed the kegs from the back of each mule. After putting the kegs in the shade, he entered the shack and filled a rusty bucket with oats. When he lifted the grain sack, a grey streak flashed under the nearest loose board. Kangaroo rats were his neighbors and housemates, and he acknowledged their presence with an occasional hurled shoe. This time he simply kicked the board with a light blow and cursed. He noticed how light the sack was and decided, after feeding what was left to the mules, to hike into Solero for supplies.

When the mules were done, he took a burlap waterbag off the wall and filled it from one of the kegs, then singled out Luke, known for his quiet company and docile nature, and looped it around his neck. He saddled the mule with a pannier to carry the supplies back from town. John, who was the noisiest of the four, complained loudly when he saw that he was not going on the trip. Matthew and Mark paid no attention to the commotion and busied themselves by chewing on a patch of stinkweed. The sun was well into its morning arc when Ashpram set out with Luke in tow, pulling gently on a length of rope. Matthew, Mark and John stared at the small cloud of dust which rose and waved and settled back into the sand behind them.

Ashpram followed a footpath running north along the rockface. Looking west, he saw Top Rock swamp like a distant oasis where the new Interstate bridged the river and fled again into the vast expanse of the white Mojave.

A red-tailed hawk circled high above, a spectral sentry at the entrance to that prehistoric canyon. After an hour he turned back to look at the range of peaks where he lived and saw the pinnacles rising up out of the topography like dark red flames. From there the journey became a tedious series of flood washes, rolling humps of sand and gravel carved by the rains as they ran off the barren mountains towards the river. Ashpram kept up an incessant dialogue, encouraging Luke with his voice, "Hup, you jackass . . . stick to the trail . . . use that peanut of a brain, Lukey, and follow me . . . hup, now . . . here's a hole for you to step in and break your leg . . . pay attention!"

They angled through the washouts and climbed the low dunes and traced the footpath parallel to the Interstate until they left the foothills completely behind. They dragged on steadily over flat terrain in the blasting noontime heat, tripping, kicking, climbing, and tumbling among the loose rocks and jumping chollas, until they came to a ditch cut by the Highway Department to ensure that any flashflood would be diverted into the river before wiping out the highway bridge. Gazing down into the man-made crevass, Ashpram was not surprised to see the rusting hulks of dead automobiles alongside dumped refrigerators, useless washing machines and various pieces of railroad debris. Luke balked at the thought of entering the trash strewn gulley, but Ashpram convinced him with one whack across his sweaty rump. The next thing he knew, Luke was parading across the eastbound lanes of I-40, snorting, reeling with truckmonster fear as one big semi after another rushed by at seventy miles-per-hour beyond the divider. Ashpram cursed and laughed at Luke's fear, but was suddenly surprised himself when he saw, cruising regally past, loaded with doors and windows and antennas, a long, silvery house on wheels. It sailed up the Top Rock offramp, and slowed to a stop, cutting its engine behind the Top Rock marina just as Ashpram and Luke entered the parking lot. The doors swung open and real children jumped out, howling and screaming as they ran towards the bewildered miner and his mildly hysterical mule.

"You see, there was these two Chinamen, Charley Quon and Lester Fat. Their grandfathers come over from China way back in the 1880's to work on the new railroad line, ended up settling out here in the Mojave Desert. Their fathers got jobs working on the same railroad and ordered their wives from some catalogue. Things were different then, you see. Anyways, the wives come to Solero and married these Chinamen and before you could say chop suey . . . all these little mail-order chinese children is running around the streets. Charley and Lester grew up together, went to the same grade school over in Essex 'cause there wasn't a schoolhouse here in those days. They were best buddies, you see. When they was old enough they went into the Army together, came back home at the same time. Their lives was just very similar, if you know what I mean. Anything Charley did, Lester had to do, and anything Lester thought up on his own, well, Charley had to copy. In fact, it would be easy to get them mixed up if they didn't look so different. Charley was a squat, rolly little Chinaman with a round friendly face and a big, bucktoothed grin, while Lester was tall and skinny and kind of gloomy-looking, with his sharp eyebrows pointed at his nose. The two of them walking side-by-side down the street was a sight to see.

"When I first met them was back in 1949, although I seen them around from time to time. They was looking to do some prospecting down in the Chocolate Mountains and sought me out for advice. Course, I never laid eyes on a sorrier pair of prospectors in my life, neither one knew which end of a pick was for digging, but they was all eager to set out and find themselves some uranium, which was what everybody was looking for in those days, and they figured I could tell them enough about the Chocolates to keep them from dying out there before they struck it rich. I can't remember whose idea this one was, but I know Charley did most of the talking and Lester only sat there, looking worried as usual. I think sometimes Lester would have liked to chuck Charley's ideas out the window and do something on his own, but he was so used to the two of them acting together and he just didn't know no other way.

"I told them what I could about the region, mostly how hard it was to find water and how bad off you would be if struck by one of them green rattlesnakes or stung by a black scorpion, but Charley just grinned like an idiot and nodded his head while old Lester looked gloomier than ever. I helped them write out a supply list, even went with them to pick out some mules from a pack ranch near Whitman, good stout brayers, from the old Tom Reed stock. Well, they bought everything they needed and then some. I didn't know you could pack so much gear onto a beast 'til I saw what those two done loaded on their mules. Hellfire, they was taking everything but the the kitchen sink, and maybe that was stuck in there somewheres, too. I mean, blankets and boxes of canned food and lanterns and shovels are all things you need in a mining camp, to be sure, but what did they need with a dozen of each? And what was they going to do with all them cameras and meters and electric gadgets they was taking along? One poor mule had a damn power generator strapped across his back and another was hauling a hydraulic drill. I tried to tell Charley you needed a powerful lot of water for that kind of operation, but he just gave me that cat-that-swallowed-the-canary smile of his and said they would be back in three months, rich as kings, don't you worry about it. Last I seen of them, they was headed south out of

Parker with Charley in the lead on a white gelding named
Caesar, twelve mules behind him and poor old Lester
bringing up the rear on a spotted pony whose name I don't
recall.

"Like I said, this was back in 1949, and all the details of
the story aren't as clear to me now as they once was.
Maybe if I had another cold beer I could remember more
about what all happened . . . why, thanky, mister.
Anyhows, I think it musta been the spring of 1950, maybe
a year or so after Lester and Charley disappeared into the
Chocolates with their two horses and twelve mules and all
that fancy gear, when I first begun to hear the rumors.
Now I don't get into town that much, maybe once every
other month or three, but when I do I like to catch up on
the news and the best place in Solero for that is the Buffalo
Nickel Saloon. They all know me there, I drink with the
Mayor and his cronies, they don't care. And you can
always find an idle drunk to tell you what's been
happening or not happening while you was gone. I can't
remember who it was informed me of this particular
occurence, coulda been Harry Hardy or or maybe even
Jack Nooncaster who was just another barfly before he
joined the Marines and came back such a bigshot hero—I
can't stand the sonuvabitch . . . but where was I? Yeah,
something had happened to the two Chinamen out there
in those mountains, something pretty awful if you
believed the talk. Some people was saying that the
Chinamen had got lucky and struck a vein of gold, then
killed each other with guns whilst fighting over shares.
Others said that Lester had finally got fed up and
murdered Charley with a pick-axe, then got lost and died
trying to get back on his own. Still another version had it
that they had found uranium after all, but had mishandled
it and both died of radiation poisoning before they could
find help. There was the usual rattlesnake versions and
mountain lion versions, too. I didn't hold stock in any of it,

but I did know one thing. In spite of all the money they spent on supplies, Charley and Lester wasn't mentally or physically fit to survive a whole year in that kind of backcountry. Besides, their original plan was to return the previous summer. Even though it was no real business of mine and I didn't owe neither of them no favors, I was just curious enough to pack a week's worth of grub on my Luke there and go have a look-see for myself. Sure, you can feed him. Carrots is fine, what he craves most is red licorice.

"Now, where was I? Oh yeah, looking for those damn two Chinamen. Figuring they wasn't the kind of men ready to go charging into the roughest country they could find, I followed the south fork of the Bill Williams River until it left the Buckskins and bled dry down around Center Wash. The traveling had to be easier for me, especially with one mule I knew instead of the twelve they didn't, and I was at the base of the Chocolates within two days. Thinking back on what I told Charley and Lester before they left, I knew there was only one of three places they could have gone. They could have continued up Center Wash to a place called Eagle's Tail, where several canyons emptied to form the mouth of the flood basin, and where a camp with access to several promising sites could be established. The danger, of course, was a sudden rain. You wouldn't think so, but we do get it from time to time. Late summer is a good a time as any. A strong thunderstorm rolling over them mountains could drop enough water inside an hour to turn Center Wash into a nasty little river. When I told Charley this he just shrugged, like flashflood wasn't a word he knew. I remember Lester didn't look so smug. Now, that was one place they could have gone and it was logical for two reasons; first, it was the simplest path to follow and the easiest place to set up camp; second, Charley, in my mind, held sway over Lester when it came to deciding whatever

the two of them was going to do, and Charley wasn't
worried about no little flashfloods. No matter his
grandaddy had seen the railroad washout near Solero in
'88 or he himself the flood that covered half of Needles
back in 1940. He was going to be rich inside of three
months and gone before summer, when the crazy weather
arrived.

"Yessir, that was a likely option, but there was two
others I had to consider. One was the Spaniard's Treasure,
a mine already dug and deserted over two centuries ago,
exact whereabouts unknown. Lester had shown me an
article from one of them adventure-seeker's magazines
describing a map, an unsolved murder, and a legendary
treasure hidden somewhere inside the mine. It wasn't the
first I had heard of the Spaniard, supposed to be worked
by California mission deserters in the mid-eighteenth
century, and it would be just like two amateur rockhounds
such as Charley and Lester to go marching into the middle
of nowhere with twelve mules, five thousand dollars
worth of mining equipment and a bogus magazine article
to find their fortunes. It was a definite possibility.

"The last place—and the least likely to consider finding
two inexperienced chinese miners a year after they
disappeared—was The Hole. I didn't bother going into
too much detail about The Hole when I first described the
area to Charley and Lester, because I was sure they
couldn't make it there. The Hole is a natural cavern sunken
into the top of the highest peak in the Chocolate range.
You can't get there without a little goat in your blood.
Taking mules and equipment is out of the question. Still, a
couple of old sappers have been known to carry out some
of the biggest gold finds this side of the Sierra Nevadas
and they claimed it was just lying there on shelfs of rock a
few hundred feet down inside the cavern, like ripe
oranges waiting to be picked. A man working alone
would have to use several hundred feet of rope and a

strong pulley to lower himself that far down, collect the goods, and then be strong enough to tow himself out again. A two-man operation would work better, but getting there was nearly impossible. The Chocolates is really just a pile of dead volcanoes eroded down to their cores, the highest point is a bare sturdy pinnacle but the crumbling flanks make the approach a risky business. I didn't see how Charley and Lester could even think of mining The Hole, no matter how big it might pay off.

"The night I camped in Center Wash, I sat up by the fire drinking coffee and mulling over where to look for what was left of the two Chinamen. I had brought a shovel along, in case they needed proper burying. I guess I hoped someone would do the same for me someday. But I sure as hell didn't have enough food or water for a long hunt. My first choice had to be the right one, or I would have to turn back no wiser then when I left. Finally, before I went to sleep, I asked Luke where he thought them dozen mules was, if they was still anywhere nearby. He looked me right in the eyes like the straight-shooter he is, and didn't say a word.

"Next morning, taking Luke's advice into consideration, of course, I made my decision and started hiking the rest of the way up Center Wash. My thinking was that Charley's confidence won out over Lester's doubts, and that they made their camp at Eagle's Tail. There had been one doozy of a rainstorm over the winter and I kept my eyes open for debris carried downwash by a flood, but I didn't see any clues, other than a rusty horseshoe that could have been there for three months or thirty years. By noon of that day I was approaching the sandy basin where the canyons converged. I seen two coyotes, a sun-drunk rattler, and a pack of ornery javelinas, but no sign that Charley and Lester came this way at all. I stopped to water Luke in the shade of a palo verde tree. I had just emptied the first of my three water

bags into a bucket when Luke's ears shot up and his
nostrils began to quiver, testing the air for something
nearby. Thinking about mountain lions—they were still
around in those days—I checked my rifle to make sure it
was loaded. About a minute later, the pinto pony came
trotting down the wash, looking ungroomed and thin,
with a wild gleam in his eyes. I whistled but he spooked
and took off up the trail at a gallop.

"It took another two hours to reach Eagle's Tail and
what was left of the Chinamen's camp. Most of the
equipment was scattered and broken to pieces, likely by
last winter's storm. I didn't see a sign of life, the pony
neither. What puzzled me was, while all the mining gear
they had brought along seemed to be there, strewn willy-
nilly down the wash for a few hundred yards, I didn't see a
single can of beans or a package of noodles anywhere.
Another thing I didn't see was any rope, but I knew for a
fact that they had hauled near a mile's worth of it up there.
While I sat there like a lump, trying to figure out what
mighta happened to two Chinamen, twelve mules, and a
hundred pounds of food, it was Luke who found the
message. I had turned him loose to graze on whatever
weeds he could find, and he sauntered away into the shade
of a gnarled old catclaw to chew on the leaves. When I
finally went over to fetch one of the water bags from off
his back, I noticed something carved into the trunk of the
tree. The letters was crude and white against the grey skin
of bark: 'Gone to the Hole, C.Q × L.F.'

"Thank you, sweetheart, Budweiser is my favorite, next
to Mexican beer. Well, I have to tell you, I couldn't believe
what I was reading! Those two musta up and abandoned
their camp, generator, drill rig, and all, and decided to
climb the highest peak in the Chocolate Mountains. It
wasn't like them to be so wasteful. I puzzled over it
awhile, then got Luke and headed up one of the finger
canyons which I knew would get me within binocular

range of the peak. I wasn't going to turn back until I knew for certain what had happened to Charley and Lester.

"That night I camped at the base of the pinnacle. It was another thousand feet to the peak, not much for your average mountain climber, but more than any miner with a mule would care to try. It was a steep rise over loose footing that became almost vertical for the last hundred yards. Like I said, it had been done a time or two before, and the stories I heard told was of a natural shaft straight down into the mountain which offered nuggets of gold assayed at 17 carats just sitting there for the picking. Charley and Lester had heard those stories, too, and my guess was that when things didn't pan out at Eagle's Tail they both got excited or desperate or both and took off for The Hole. The only question in my mind was whether or not they was still alive. It wasn't likely, considering how long they had been gone, but I wanted some kind of evidence, maybe just an old hat or an empty water can, to take back to their folks in town.

"Next morning, I set out with some crackers and water and a pair of binoculars tied up in a knapsack, along with a good length of rope and a miner's lamp belted around my waist, leaving Luke and the rest of my grub at camp. I hiked over the first pile of boulders until I came to the small crumbling slate that made the climb such a hazard. From there I had a pretty good vantage point, both for studying the peak with my glasses and for looking back down the valley. I decided to stay put and enjoy the weather. It was a cool dry day and the air was clear as new glass. On days like that you could see fifty miles across the desert, if you was standing in the right place. I have to admit, the view was so fine that I didn't pay much attention as to the peak. It wasn't until around noon that I caught a glimpse of something moving up there, but I couldn't be sure—was it a man or a mountain sheep? After that I kept my eyes glued to the binocs and aimed at the peak. It wasn't long before I saw the figure of a man walking along the horizon, a tall skinny man that very well could have been Lester Fat. Now I had no choice. I was going to climb to The Hole myself to see what the hell was going on up there.

"I won't go into all the details of that climb, only to say I nearly fell off the mountain twice and almost turned back when I was no more than fifty feet from the peak, but I finally dragged myself wheezing and sweating and cursing over the edge. When I stood up and beat the dust out of my clothes and hat, nobody was there to greet me. The top of the mountain was a flat piece of lava rock maybe thirty feet wide at any point. On all sides the drop was vertical. Nobody could have gotten down any easier than I had just come up. So where had the man I saw through the binocs disappeared to? Only one place. There in the middle of that desolate rock was The Hole. It was not a big gap. I reckon you might have dropped a small truck down it if you were somehow able to get one up there. I stayed as quiet as possible while walking over to the edge to look down into it. I couldn't see much, the sun was at a low angle and only the first ten feet or so was in light, but I felt the cold draft coming out of it and smelled the raw sulfur stink and I knew it was a good long drop to the bottom.

"Now I'm no braver than the next man, but if there's one thing I am it's stubborn. Once I set myself to a particular job or idea, there ain't much in this world that can sway me. Must be the company I keep. And I was bound and determined to find out what happened to those two Chinamen. There was only one thing to do. I lashed my rope around a firm outcrop near the lip of The Hole and using a few knots learned from my Navy days, lowered myself down into the darkness on the belay, with my miner's lamp flashing against the wall in front of me, flushing out an occasional bat. I must have gone down close to one hundred feet, because I was about at the end of my line, when the light from my lamp shone on an opening in the rock. So far I had seen nothing but the natural formation of the shaft, but this was different. Somebody had made this gap with tools, working in from a ledge of slick greenish stone. I could see a vein of green between the manmade cracks. From the condition of the excavated wall I judged the dig was recent. The gravel left behind looked fresh and uneroded. Somebody had been digging here, probably not long ago. I lowered myself further, and, with my lamp pointed straight down, I saw I was coming to a kind of floor or ledge where the shaft changed direction and went off at an angle into the flank of the mountain. My rope ran out before I was quite to the floor. I was dangling about ten feet above it, studying the foothold below me with my lamp. I figured I could drop myself out of the belay without breaking a leg, but I didn't see how I was gonna get ahold of the rope again, since it would be way above my reach once I got down there. Then I thought of something. By unbuckling my belt and strapping it to the end of the line I could lower myself another three feet, enough to drop to the ground easily and put me within jumping reach of the rope when I needed it again. I hit the ground with a thud, nearly broke the damn lamp, but I was okay and the lamp still worked, so I took a good look around to see what I was into. Water was dripping from above, probably coming from the crack I had noticed before. This made the rock floor slippery and hard to walk on. The shaft made a break at this point, turning into the side of the mountain but still going down at a steep angle. It would be one iffy ride trying to follow it without a rope. There was something else, too. Once again, somebody had been busy digging and this time they had made some real headway because the shaft made a detour and went straight ahead on level footing further than my lamp could shine. I decided that was the way to go. I walked ahead slowly, careful not to slip on the wet floor. I hadn't gone far before I heard something, a distant pounding of steel on rock. I was getting closer to the answer to my questions. My lamp grew weaker and then petered out altogether, probably from being thrown against the ground, but funny enough I could see better without it. Stumbling and tripping down the manmade shaft, I realized I was approaching daylight. Rounding a bend in the cavern, I came into bright afternoon sunshine. An opening maybe five feet in diameter pointed out toward the western skyline. And the ringing sound of hammer on stone grew even louder. I ran the last twenty steps into the open, and almost fell to my death, God's truth. That was good and cold, do you have another, just one more?

"Hot out here, ain't it though? So there I was, on a ledge no more than three feet wide hanging on the opposite side of the mountain I had climbed up all afternoon. That's why I hadn't see the opening before. To my left, working like a maniac with his woodhandled miner's axe was Lester Fat. And a few feet past him, sure enough, was the skeleton of Charley Quon sitting by himself on a kind of volcanic throne, looking west with empty sockets open wide. Lester didn't seem to recognize me, or at least he didn't bother to acknowledge my presence. He just kept digging. After I had given him some time to get used to me being there, I went over beside Lester and sat down. It was then I noticed he was shivering, probably with hunger or thirst or both. I took some crackers and water from my bag and tried to offer them to him. Lester just kept digging. I wasn't planning on spending the night up there, so I got right to the point and asked him what had happened. Why did they leave Eagle's Tail? What was Charley doing over there, dead as he was? How had he managed to survive all this time in The Hole without any food? My questions all came tumbling out while poor

Lester was down on his knees, with that blank look of his, glancing over at Charley now and then while he swung the pick into the mountainside, as if he was still taking orders. Then he took in a deep breath, sighed, and began to sob. It was that silent, tearless kind of crying that tells you when a man is hurt too deep for words. I decided not to push him any further, but it was getting dark and he wasn't showing any sign of slowing down. I sat up with poor Lester half the night while he continued his digging, until my own exhaustion took over and I fell into a troubled sleep.

"I awoke the next morning to the sound of Lester's hammer, and I realized he had gone plumb crazy, over gold or food or the heat, I didn't know which. I wondered if he had dug the shaft I walked through all himself by hand. I decided he probably had. I surmised they had gone down into the Hole and had been unable to climb out again, and so had dug towards from the side of the mountain. I decided the job had been so hard and taken so long they had both cracked under the strain. And I was mostly right. Before I left him there, Lester spoke to me. He didn't say much, but it was enough to tell me things had been hard for him since Charley died.

" 'He shouldn't of eaten that white horse,' he said. He was looking at Charley's skeleton when he said it. 'Never shoulda done that. Them mules warn't so bad . . . but that white horse didn't set right with him.'

" 'Why don't you come home with me, Lester?' I said.

"He shook his head and commenced to digging. 'I got work to do,' he told me, 'More than I know what to do with.'

"There was something in his voice that told me it was useless to argue, maybe even fatal. He still had that pick in his hand when I left him there.

"This is my guess. They had lived off mule meat for a year and then were down to the horse and pony. Lester had let his pony go because he couldn't see clear to eat it, but Charley had killed and butchered his own horse without a qualm. Of all the things Charley had done in spite of Lester, this musta been the worse. It broke Lester's spirit. Later, when things had gone black and they couldn't climb out, he killed Charley and cannibalized his body, and with that terrible food fueled his digging a cave through the side of the mountain. I could tell from how clean the skeleton was. The sun and wind and rain takes much longer to pick us clean. You need buzzards and crows to really shine like Charley did. I figured all this out while climbing back down the mountain. Going down was easy. I found the basecamp where they had tethered the animals and done the butchering and cooking. I reached my own bottom camp that afternoon and began the hike out with Luke before sundown. We traveled all night and were back home before the next nightfall. I told their folks I didn't know what happened for sure, but I supposed it was a flashflood got 'em. I gave their families some of the things they had abandoned at Eagle's Tail, a few clothes, some steel pans, and left the rest of the story alone. Until now."

Luke was more patient than a buzzard, more durable than a pony, and more tolerant than a grandfather, carrying each abusive child around the gravel parking lot in steady monotonous circles. Ashpram collected money from the doting parents who followed him with cameras and road maps and questions about the mine. He fascinated them, describing the lode of silver he discovered near Whitman in 1927, the rare topaz he unearthed above Butler's Wash during the Depression, his unbelievable gold find outside Borax in 1944. He showed them his yellow crowns and turquoise belt-buckle. He drew maps in the sand of mines that did not exist. He sweated and swore and took the money in, dollar by dollar, wrinkling them into his jeans and imploring Luke to return for the next ride, as if the mule were no more than a silenced partner in some covert manipulation of the tourist industry, his tail working methodically against the flies. Each child was carried back, wide-eyed and exuberant, galloping in some childhood fantasy of horses and deserts and swords, while their mothers looked to catch them from falling and their fathers stared at the Colorado River running under the bridge, trying to imagine how that much snow could fall so far way and still travel here, clear and blue and cold, through the technological grace of the Department of the Interior.

When Aspram had taken in his last dollar, the owner of the boat marina came screaming about the loss of business and the donkey chips in his driveway. Ashpram slipped him a fiver and there was peace. Luke retired into the shade of the cottonwoods to munch on green stalks of celery given to him by the children. Their parents offered Ashpram whiskey which he declined and wine which he disdained and beer which he loved, so he accepted a sixpack and went to a table on the porch of the marina to drink it. He continued to lie to whomever was listening about everything from his income to his age to the ability of mules to become bilingual. The tourists recognized the lies for what they were and laughed and drank and clicked pictures of him that they would take home to show their neighbors in Spokane and Toledo and St.Paul.

Thickened by heat and alcohol, the flow of memories slowed to a trickle. The boomtown recollections became melancholoy as Ashpram related them to his audience of retired insurance agents and their wives. The stories grew sullen, peopled by ghosts existing in empty towns where the livelihoods had melted as fluidly as snow and driven men to fates of hermitage and seclusion. He talked of hidden caches unfound to this day, of murders and madness and treachery, all for the love of gold, his words beginning to slur with beer breath as he coughed into his dirty sleeve and tried to keep the salty beads of sweat from stinging his eyes. The tales became morbid, preposterous, unreal. He awoke from their telling like a sleepwalker, confused and suspicious of where he had been. He mumbled something about the danger of riverside diamondbacks, frightening an Indiana housewife into spanking her innocent child for wandering off towards the shoreline. That sobering spectacle convinced Ashpram that he needed to get his supplies and leave.

He loaded the panniers and strapped them across Luke's back, then escaped the small crowd of tourists by walking under the railroad bridge. Two curious boys followed him out to the highway. He waved and pointed to the jagged range of stone teeth lying in wait for him, a few miles to the south. The boys leaned together as he disappeared into the labyrinth of canyons and flood ravines leading back into the Big Marias. They hesitated a moment, then returned to the safety of the parking lot where the marina owner stood, cursing Ashpram under his breath and shovelling up the big mess that Luke had left behind.

*A*n official California township was registered by a group of confused Mormons who became beached while seeking a steamship passage between southern Utah and the Sea of Cortez. Addled by the heat and without the resources to return to Salt Lake City, they befriended the Moabis, temporarily converted them to the worship of Nephi, and built a row of sheds and cabins out of lumber salvaged from the stranded steamboat.

They wrote a letter to the Governor in Provo who forwarded it to his counterpart in Sacramento and their request for official recognition was granted. The town was called Solero, a name derived from the Mormons' innate misunderstanding of local geology and the Spanish language.

The Mormons lasted a little more than a decade, growing beans, eating dogfish and singing their strange ethereal hymns. Unfortunately, several years of drought in the distant Rockies gradually parched the lower river and each day the town grew further away from the waterline. They were finally forced to pack up and leave on foot without ever realizing their dream of establishing a commercial steamship route between Solero and the port of Guaymas on the Mexican mainland.

# Welcome to Nowhere

---

The current location of Solero was a road map mystery. The Highway Department denied the existence of any wrongdoing, but the foremen and road workers saw the truth written in the plans they carried out daily. The grey cement river they were pouring, an Interstate business loop four lanes wide across thirty-six miles of the Sonora-Mojave basin, bypassed the little river town in favor of more level terrain a few miles to the south, cutting directly through the northwest corner of the Moabi Indian Reservation.

It would have been simple enough to redirect the proposed route during the first stages of desk top planning, but hundreds of thousands of tax dollars were already invested in right-of-way acquisitions and soil erosion tests and offramp specification blueprints. When a civil engineer back at Department headquarters finally recognized just how badly he had missed the mark, mistaking an abandoned cavalry fort for downtown Solero on the aerial survey chart, a meeting of mid-level bureaucrats was held. It was decided to save money and move the town instead. This happened suddenly, without prior warning, like a late summer flashflood.

The Army Corps of Engineers was nearly done with the bridge at Top Rock. Working in conjunction with the Bureau of Reclamation, they had temporarily diverted the river, forming a wide swamp on the Arizona side where the surface of the once turbulent Colorado became flat and murky, like an antique mirror. The bridge itself was supported by huge abutments which were lowered into the vacant riverbed with towering radial boom cranes. Reinforced concrete set in wide interlocking spans gave the bridge a look of stark, utilitarian power. Its completion would mark the end of a nine-year-long project, allowing Interstate traffic to splinter away from old Route 66 a dozen miles south of Kingman and angle westward through a range of low, rust-colored volcanics. The ambitious roadcut had taken thirty tons of dynamite, sixteen million dollars and the lives of two men. It was designed to shave forty-five minutes off the Kingman-Barstow drive. Perched on the bare limbs of drowned cottonwood trees at the southern end of the swamp, a flock of blue herons faced the oncoming construction with a natural indifference.

Late that summer, a small plane carrying state architects arrived one afternoon from Sacramento, landing on a crude runway that had not existed one week earlier. They were met by an unmarked Highway Department van and shuttled to a pink motel just across the Nevada border where, invigorated by the arid night breeze, they played cards and drank vodka until dawn. The next morning, sleepless, unshaven, and without remorse for the previous night's debauchery, they drove out to the project headquarters a few miles west of Solero. They came unprepared for the intense rigors of the daytime desert. By nine o'clock it was too hot to walk outside without a hat on; an hour later, most of the architects were sick to their stomachs and badly dehydrated; by noon, all work had ground to a halt and the state crew was holed up inside a portable bungalow, quaffing ice water and vomitting into white plastic bags provided by a kindhearted engineer.

The head foreman, a heavyset ex-Marine named Jack Nooncaster, studied the suffering public servants silently. He had spent the last five years overseeing the highway's fate, and was so close to coming in on time and under budget that he had already spent the bonus money on a new Mustang convertible. Nooncaster had been a sergeant in Korea decorated for valor and was something of a local hero. During his military career, he had learned the value of a calculated impatience. He sat in his cramped little trailer office, looking at survey maps and smoking a cigar in grim silence. A black labrador retriever rested obediently at his feet. He was waiting until just the right moment, when the architects were beginning to show signs of recovery. He looked into the next room and saw that they were out of danger, some of them even joking about the lovely weather. He then stepped into the room, cleared his throat and addressed the group. Using his worst bootcamp English, Nooncaster threatened to have them all removed from their airconditioned offices at department headquarters and reassigned to supervise a series of projected roadcuts through the Panamint Range in Death Valley, guaranteeing they would be required to work long hours outdoors right alongside the flaggers, blasters and bulldozer crews until their ears went bad from too many dynamite concussions and their eyes burned out from solar radiation and their skins turned into something the texture of tortoise leather, while their wives shacked up with the local uranium miners and their children ran wild with roving packs of coyotes, whereupon he cracked a six-pack out of his personal beer cooler and pointed them towards the door, handing each flushed bureaucrat a cold one as they went back out into the quaking noonday heat. Then and there, without benefit of proper surveys, the group of hungover draftsmen made a series of on-the-spot drawings which put the town of Solero three miles west of where it had ever been before, and precisely where Nooncaster wanted it, at the new junction of I-40 and Old Highway 95.

When they were done, Nooncaster said thanks, gave each man another beer before dinner, and sent them all packing back to the Governor with a sealed envelope which contained his private environmental impact report, all the authorized inspection signatures, and an anonymous donation to the re-election funds. He immediately ordered one of his maintenance crews to move the town's welcome sign out to the new site and had another man plant some nursery-grown palms nearby. Then he took the retriever and went duck hunting in the swampy growth north of the bridge.

Within the week a company of bulldozers had flattened the surrounding landscape. Soon thereafter, a huge shipment of cinderblocks and rebar steel arrived via the railroad. The yardmen, mostly Indians from the reservation supervised by union bosses, worked overtime in the afternoon heat unloading the heavy freight from the baking cars and placing it on flatbed trucks for the five-mile ride out to the site of the new Highway Department compound, which was going up rapidly near the proposed Interstate offramp. At about the same time, property agents representing franchise interests from Chicago, St. Louis and New York descended on the area like a flock of roadside crows. Realtors from Los Angeles and Phoenix flew in with attractive land deals enveloped inside their vinyl leather briefcases. These clandestine offers were laid on the table at a special meeting of local developers and hastily accepted by the tribal advisory council, the two groups being one and the same bunch of asthmatic dentists, pensioned war veterans and railroad officials due for an early retirement. Indian land was still going cheap in 1969 and so was their future.

*T*he railroad arrived in the late 1880's.

A narrowing of the river near Top Rock (an English corruption of the original Moabi name) made the area a strategic crossing point. Jobs building and maintaining a bridge for the Atchison, Topeka and Santa Fe line attracted several hundred Chinese immigrants into the region. Across the river on the California shore, the town of Solero grew rapidly with the construction of a railroad office, courthouse and jail under the protection of nearby Fort Mojave.

The town was nearly erased from the map in 1902, when the river changed course overnight and moved three miles to the east. This was not unusual in the pre-dam era, when the fickle waters of the Colorado were known to meander, often branching into two or more channels and wandering for miles over flat terrain. Eventually, the river returned, forking around the growing town in hazardous floodstreams which threatened to erase whatever human progress had been made in their absence. Fearing a repetitive chain of natural disasters, the railroad transferred its regional headquarters to Barstow.

After the flood, the town began a long slow decline that lasted for the next thirty years. Oldtimers died, whole families moved away and the population, which at the height of the boom had approached ten thousand souls, dwindled to less than five hundred. Buildings sat empty along Main Street, haunted only by the whistling wind. The courthouse was boarded up. So were the post office and barber shop, the incessant wind and sun eating slowly at their wooden falsefronts.

# The Night Raven Stole the Moon

Harry Hardy worked the graveyard shift in a coffee shop out along the new Interstate business loop. SAMBO'S stood at the far western edge of town, facing a section of concrete highway that jumped the last wash and veered suddenly away into the white miles of open desert. It was the only place in Solero still busy after midnight that didn't serve booze, sell gas, or pretend to massage your neck.

Harry cooked on short order, eleven to seven. The kitchen was his until five in the morning when two Arabs came in to help prepare for the breakfast rush. He liked to arrive early, maybe ten-thirty or a quarter 'til, to sit at the clean formica counter and rest his booted feet after the long walk down Main Street, past the bars and the railyards and the Highway Department compound. He sipped lukewarm coffee and listened with vacant curiosity to the talk of passing truckers.

Tanned, muscular men with bold tattoos, they crowded into the narrow booths to exchange road news and compare their superior engines, their impressive payloads, their coast-to-coast methedrine marathons. They all seemed to possess the same diesel-loud voices, the same downshifting, throaty laughter. Harry listened silently, tasting the stale dregs of swingshift coffee while he nursed a secret envy. The truckers chided and cursed each other, repeating vulgar accounts of what happened in El Paso over the weekend, who caught a certain disease in Albuquerque, how friendly a female hitchhiker was outside of Tucson, while Harry sat alone at the end of the counter with his apron and baggy chef's hat, trying to remember the last time he had ventured as far north as Las Vegas, less than ninety miles away.

That night, sitting by himself per usual and staring vacantly at the clock on the wall, Harry got the uncomfortable feeling someone was standing close behind him.

"How's it?" a man's voice blasted into his ear, a gruff baritone that wrenched Harry from the quicksand of solitude. "You supposed to be the cook here or somethin'?"

"Yeah," Harry turned, guardedly, as if expecting a blow to the head.

"Well, what's good to eat around here besides waitress burgers?" The loud voice belonged to a burly, blackhaired biker. He wore a wool skullcap, black leather jacket, and oilstained blue jeans tucked into heavy parachute boots laced half way to his knees. A long and snarled ponytail swung behind him. He took off the jacket and draped it over the back of the stool, revealing thick and sinewy arms decorated from shoulder to wrist with dark green tattoos. As he took a seat beside him at the counter, Harry noticed that the raw, meaty hands which reached for the menu were covered with grease.

"Danny Breedlove," the biker rasped, catching his breath as he let out a belch, "from San Berdoo."

"Pleased to meet you," said Harry, nervously swirling the grinds in the bottom of his cup.

The biker smiled, exposing teeth the color of wet cigarettes. "Harry, huh?" The name was printed on the clownish hat that the manager made all the cooks wear.

"That's what they call me around here," Harry grinned uncomfortably.

"The Chain. That's what the Ravens call me."

"The ravens?"

"Yeah, you know, the Ravens. They're my people. You seen us, sure, little bike club out of San Berdoo?"

Harry nodded slowly, didn't say anything.

"You seen us, man, come on. Twelve bad dudes ridin' Harleys?" He looked at Harry for an earnest response, an affirmation of the Ravens great notoriety in Solero. "Sure, you seen us. We cross this desert like it was our backyard, man. We got maps of it scratched into our eyelids. We ride without lights when the moon is shining."

"Well, yeah, I heard about this one fella," Harry agreed politely, "who was riding his motor-sickle by the light of the moon on the I-40 out of Barstow. They say he musta been going 'bout a hundred and twenty miles per when he hit that stalled Greyhound. Just plain disintegrated. The Marines claim they saw the fireball clear out to Twenty-nine Palms."

The biker turned away without speaking and studied the menu closely. With one hand he brushed the road dust from his dark eyebrows, and with the other he pointed at different glossy pictures of salads, soups, and hamburger plates. After a minute, he looked back at Harry.

"So you live here, huh? Here in Sombrero?"

"Solero," Harry corrected, his eyes straying automatically towards the clock above the swinging metal door which led to the kitchen.

"Then maybe you can tell me somethin' I've always wondered about this place."

"I'd be happy to tellya," said Harry, "only I gotta be to work in 'bout thirty seconds, and from the way you been lookin' at that menu . . . you wouldn't want me to be late."

The biker looked directly at Harry for the first time, studying the apron and chef's hat and pointed cowboy boots. Pulling the skullcap up over his ears and off, he itched the stubble of beard on his chapped face and shook his head in obvious discomfort.

"Is it true?" the Chain wanted to know.

Harry lifted his mug and stood as if to leave.

"Is it true?" he repeated, "I mean, what they say about the women in this town?"

"What do they say?" Harry wondered aloud.

"Is it true the women out here do it like jackrabbits?"

Harry finished his coffee and pushed through the swinging door at eleven o'clock sharp. A backlog of orders was already tacked on a revolving chrome wheel above the wide aluminum ledge where all ready-to-serves were placed. The cook coming off duty, a seventeen-year-old runaway from Phoenix named Bruce, always managed to step out the back door for a smoke during the last five minutes of his shift, leaving the graveyard man plenty to catch up on. Harry never complained to the management. Tonight he simply rolled up his sleeves, retied his apronstrings, and went to work on three cheeseburgers, a Denver omelette, and a bowl of chile con carne.

"Hi, Harry."

"Mornin', Grace."

Grace Johnson worked week nights and Saturdays, part time. Her husband was a welder for the Atchison-Topeka and was often gone on a bridge or track repair for two or three weeks at a time. She was a shy girl, with smooth fragile features and slim delicate limbs. Although he knew she didn't really belong there, Harry enjoyed her youthful company in the slow, time-killing hours between two a.m. and dawn, when the rest of town went to sleep and the truckers climbed back behind their wheels and the coyotes came out in roving packs to howl at the moon.

"Looks like Bruce didn't bother saying goodbye again tonight." Grace leaned over the ledge to take a cheeseburger and fries plate.

"Naw," Harry smiled. "Probably already back in his motel room with a sixpack on the table, playing that damn guitar."

"He has a nice voice," Grace said. "I heard him sing once. A real pretty country song."

"I bet he does." The grill sizzled and spit at Harry's hands as he flipped the patties. "Grace, honey? Could you ask Dottie about this order? Ask her what the hell is a BLT N/C? Ask her for me, wouldya?" Grace giggled and went away with the combo.

Dottie Smith drew more than giggles from most people. A buxom blonde with a towering B-52 hairdo and an ample bosom, Dottie had been waiting tables before Grace was born. She had worked her way west over the past twenty years through a series of bad marriages, only to find herself at the unforgiving age of thirty-nine stranded in the middle of the Mojave Desert with two young sons, a rusty station wagon and a trailer home won in her last divorce settlement. Although she was popular with the truckers for her volatile temper and occasional outbursts of junkyard language, she talked too much, couldn't add or subtract with any degree of accuracy, and gave Harry heartburn trying to decode her gradeschool scribblings. Her main ambition in life was to make it to San Diego for Christmas.

After Grace went off to look for her, Harry got down to business. He took a bag of precut potatoes from the freezer and dumped the contents into a wire basket, which he lowered into a trough of bubbling grease. He spread out a stack of hamburger patties on the grill and the meat started to cook with an angry, snapping sound. As the patties began to bulge with hot juice, Harry flattened them with a spatula, and the grill sizzled even louder. He diced wedges of onions and tomatoes and prepared the garnishes for upcoming orders, working steadily with a dogged expression upon his wrinkled face. He was brushing butter over bread buns and turning them face down to toast when Grace reappeared at the order window.

"Bacon, lettuce, tomato, no cheese," she said.

"No cheese? Is that what she wrote?" Harry sighed, "Geezus, I never put cheese on a BLT in my life."

Grace put on a fresh pot of coffee. Harry bent over the hot grill, a ring of moisture already darkening the white rim of his hat. He reached for plates, loaded them with food, and whisked them across the metal ledge where they sat steaming until Dottie or Grace came to take them away. The order window gave him a framed view of the restaurant as he worked. Peering between the malt shaker and the stainless steel pie cabinet, Harry could follow the random movements of the crowd. At the moment, a salesman stood with his sample case at the cash register studying a map of California. Two off-duty brakemen talked baseball in a booth near the door. The greasy biker was still seated alone at the counter, picking at his salad and reading the song selector in front of him with a bored expression.

"Harry, sweetie."

"Don't sweetie me," Harry growled as Dottie's face materialized before him. "What is this about no cheese on a BLT? You know I don't put cheese on a BLT!"

Dottie threw back her head and cackled like a hen. She was chewing gum, her bobbing cheeks pink with rouge, her heavily mascaraed eyes crinkling with mischief.

"I dunno," said Dottie with a shrug.

"I dunno," Harry mimed. "Geezus Christ!"

"Don't you swear at me, Harry Hardy!" Dottie spit. "Some guy at table sixteen told me he didn't want cheese on his BLT. Simple as that. He said to be sure to tell the cook, no cheese, especially American. He hates American cheese, Harry. Simple as that. You don't have to swear at me, for godsakes."

Harry stood there looking sheepish. He noticed that the biker was listening to the conversation and seemed to be enjoying it more than his salad.

"Sorry, Dottie, I didn't mean to . . ."

"You give her hell, Harry," boomed the Chain.

Dottie smiled coyly, smacked her chewing gum, and scooped four plates onto one arm. "Who's your friend, Harry?" she asked before leaving.

Harry went back to work without answering her, glaring sullenly down at the grill as he scraped it clean for the next batch of patties. He was embarassed at being so closely observed by one of the customers, especially a roughneck like the Chain. Luckily, things were so busy that he didn't have time to worry about it much. A group of Indians who worked nights in the railyards came in for their usual midnight lunch break. Grace corralled the eight of them into two booths at the back of the coffee shop and took their orders. Dottie often commented on how their orders hardly varied from one day to the next, and how it was a waste of time bothering to ask them what they wanted. In typical fashion she got down to business, insulting the wily truckdrivers, making fun of the crewcut young Marines, and giving absolute hell to the overweight highway engineers who stopped at SAMBO'S after hitting the Rainbow Room or the Buffalo Nickel Saloon for a few beers. Grace moved back and forth behind her like an efficient shadow, making sure each meal arrived at its intended destination and was still hot enough to be eaten without complaint.

"I need more patties," Harry yelled. "Gracie? They're back in the deep-freeze under the fish sticks. Could you fetch me about four dozen?"

Grace disappeared through the rear kitchen door, which led to a walk-in pantry and a large storage freezer. Out front, three more men came into the restaurant. Harry recognized them as Mexican farmworkers from one of the irrigation projects near Parker. They stood uncertainly in the glassed-in vestibule, waiting to be seated. After a couple of minutes, Dottie came over and showed them to the counter, right beside the Chain and directly in front of Harry's window. She got them each a glass of ice water and a menu, then waltzed over to waste a few minutes bending Harry's ear.

"Hold the lettuce for those three, whatever they order." She dropped her tablet on the ledge and lit a smoke. "I bet they're sick of looking at it. I need seven cheebies and a chili for the tribe."

"No more patties," Harry said. "I sent Grace back . . ."

"Harry, did I ever tell you what that creep from Yuma did to me?"

"No, and I don't care to hear it, Dottie."

"You know, the one who claimed to own a beach house on Balboa Island."

"Never had the pleasure."

"Yes you did. He was the one with the pink Cadillac, the one who promised to get me out of this firehole by next June. God, you'd think it was June already instead of only April. I bet it was one hundred degrees by noon today."

This happened every night, at the height of the midnight rush, when Harry was at his busiest and the whole place was buzzing with hungry, talkative men.

Dottie would stop everything, light a cigarette, and list the many problems of her life in Solero. No matter what Harry said or did to discourage the conversation, she carried it on until the subject was exhausted or her cigarette went out, whichever came first. The list was endless: her string of worthless ex-husbands, her lack of money, her two young boys (one of them was retarded), her insomnia, and her adamant disdain for the sinister desert heat. Harry thought it rather peculiar that, although she could not stand the soaring temperatures of the local climate, she never made arrangements to leave. After four and a half years, he was tired of hearing about it. Whenever she brought up the subject of weather, he reminded her it was better living here than in Alaska, where he had seen military service during World War II.

"Alaska?" she chided. "Who ever lived in Alaska?"

"Me. For three goddam years. No sun. No women. Nothing. And enough snow to start another ice age."

"Aw, come off it, Harry. The only duty you ever saw was on television."

"Hey, Harry," the Chain joined in too loudly. "Would you know what to do with a woman if they had one up there in Alaska?"

"Who is this grease gorilla?" Dottie wheeled around to glare at the biker.

The Chain bared his brown smile, lasciviously eyeing the waitress from head to toe. "You know me, babe, I'm one of the Ravens."

Dottie stubbed out the cigarette, picked up her tablet, and turned to address Harry, who was watching the biker warily. "Where's that Grace?" she demanded. "Am I gonna go it alone tonight?"

"I don't know," Harry mumbled. "She went in the back."

Grace came up behind him with two packets of fish sticks. Harry looked down at them and then up at Grace. Her eyes were red and puffy from crying.

"Grace? Those aren't hamburger patties, hon."

"Oh, I'm sorry, Harry. I thought this is what you . . ." She backed away from Harry with the fish sticks in her hands and turned away towards the freezer in the storeroom, sniffling as she went.

"What was that all about?" asked Dottie.

Harry shrugged, "Search me."

Harry was often at a loss to understand the complex emotions of his female co-workers. His daily proximity to women like Grace and Dottie made him the butt of jokes among his drinking buddies at the Buffalo Nickel Saloon, yet he remained as compassionate and understanding as he could manage to be. Wondering to himself what he might have done that hurt Grace enough to make her cry, Harry dropped a steak over the grill fire. Flames leapt wildly for an instant and subsided just as quickly while the smoke they created curled up through the bars and stung his eyes.

The orders quickly backed up, due not only to Grace's breakdown but also to Dottie's ill-timed cigarette break. Harry worked at a frenzied pace for the next half-hour. When Grace came back with the patties, her eyes were dried, but she held her head down, averting Harry's questioning gaze. There were men waiting in booths who hadn't ordered yet, and she hurried off to see to them. Harry's hands and legs shifted into automatic as he spun around the grill and kitchen area, flipping burgers, dicing more onions, ladling out chili and soup, preparing plates and side dishes, the sweat streaming down his brow and dripping off the end of his nose. He lost track of everything but his work, which helped time pass, if nothing else.

Before he knew it, the restaurant had emptied and the
clock was pushing one in the morning. Thursday night
had crossed the border of loneliness into another early
Friday. Dottie came over with her cigarettes and Harry
decided he could take a break himself. It was then that he
noticed the Chain was still there, keeping his hawklike
eyes trained on Grace as she moved between the tables,
meticulously wiping down and resetting each place with
silverware.

Harry scattered some french fries on a plate and placed
them up on the ledge where he and Dottie could share
them. He got his own cigarettes from a cubbyhole near the
swinging door and pulled one out. Dottie stood between
the counter and the order window, blowing smoke
towards the ceiling and nibbling at an occasional fry,
watching the Chain as he followed Grace's movements
around the coffee shop.

"Your friend likes what he sees," she said to Harry when
he walked up to the window. "I think Grace had better
look out tonight."

"Yeah," Harry nodded, "I wonder if Wayne is home."

Dottie shook her head, "Don't think so. She said
something about a job up in Sacramento Wash. Wayne
would be staying in Kingman 'til next Sunday."

"Oh," Harry's voice was small and distant.

Dottie turned to look at him, smiling at his worried
expression, "Harry? Are you feeling like a big brother or
something? She's a not a little girl. She can take care of
herself."

"I know, but I don't like the looks of that fellow. Not a
bit."

The Chain, just out of earshot, looked over at Dottie
and Harry, then stood up and moved down the counter
towards them. For the first time Harry noticed he was
wearing a buck knife in a black scabbard on his hip. He sat
down in front of them and placed both grease-stained

hands on the counter, like a card player waiting for his deal.

"Harry," he said in his overloud tone, "I'm still wonderin', is it true what they say?"

Harry gulped a few more french fries and washed them down with coffee, then cleared his throat and spoke. "If you're done with your meal, I think you'd better leave."

The Chain looked at him quizzically, a furrow of sunburned skin knotting his thick brow.

"I think you had better just move on down the road," Harry repeated, keeping his voice as even as possible, "and don't come back."

A dark cloud settled in behind the Chain's eyes, unleashing an electrical storm which caused his face to glow purple in the coffee shop light. One of the soiled hands slipped down to his hip and unjacketed the bonehandled knife. He brought it out slowly, deliberately, with a furious calm, his glare fastened on Harry, and laid it down on the yellow counter before him.

"Look, bud," Dottie spoke up, carelessly stubbing her cigarette into the tray beside him, less than six inches from the knife, "we don't want any trouble here. If you want me to fix you a cup of coffee, it's on the house. Now, put that pigsticker away before you cut yourself and . . ."

"Shut up, bitch," said the Chain, his black eyes rivetted to the order window and ignoring Dottie completely.

The trouble had started before Harry knew what was happening. He heard Grace scream and grabbed the nearest weapon. He came out through the swinging doors with a long, gleaming butcher knife in his hand. Dottie and the Chain were faced off over two broken dishes with scraps of half-eaten food sprinkled at their feet. Shredded bits of lettuce, tomato and pickle were hanging from the front of the Chain's leather jacket, and he held the buck knife pointed towards her stomach.

"Call me that again," Dottie snarled, " . . . and I'll scratch your eyes out and give them to Harry for the morning hash."

When the Chain saw Harry with the butcher knife his look of dark fury was replaced by a wary agitation. At that moment, the glass doors in the vestibule swung open and an old Indian walked in carrying a limp burlap sack. The Chain looked at the old man over his shoulder, then back at Harry, who had come around the corner and was standing in the lane between the counter and the wall.

"You had better go right now," Harry said, "before you get into something you can't handle." He could hear himself speak, but didn't recognize his own voice.

The Chain smiled then. He was holding the buck knife about two feet from Dottie's belly. A quick thrust would have disembowelled her. But he just stood there, grinning at Harry, shaking his head from side to side.

"You lied to me, Harry. You don't know anything about the Ravens. If you did, you wouldn't be trying to pull this shit on me."

"I don't see any Ravens," said Harry.

"No," the Chain answered, "they're hard to see at night, but they're out there. I promise you that."

The Indian, Johnny Earth Tongue, walked up to the counter as if nothing in the world was wrong, and took a seat near the door. The smell of alcohol followed him into the restaurant. Although his posture was stiff and erect, his movements were sluggish and his eyes had a glazed, faraway expression.

"Is this fella from your gang, Harry?" the Chain smirked, lowering the knife and sliding the blade back into its sheath. "The Chickens?"

"Harry wouldn't need a gang to take care of the likes of you," Dottie hissed.

Harry shook his head, "Be quiet, Dottie. He's leaving."

"That's right, I am," the Chain nodded, "but I'll be back later . . . with the Ravens."

Dottie laughed, "Oh, god! I'm shaking all over."

As he turned to leave, the Chain looked over at Grace, who was standing behind Dottie, clutching a red dustrag to her chest. She stared down at the linoleum tile, not wanting to meet his leering eyes.

"I'll be back for you, sweet meat," he said, "so don't worry." He spit on the floor at Dottie's feet, then rammed through the swinging door and out into the night. A moment later, a motorcycle blasted angrily to life in the parking lot, and there was the high-pitched whine of the engine racing away to the west.

"Let's call the Sheriff," said Dottie.

"Naw, let him go," Harry was watching Grace bend to pick up the broken plates. "He won't be back."

"How do you know?"

"I just do. The Highway Patrol will be in for breakfast around five. We'll tell them what happened and they can take care of it."

Harry went back into the kitchen. He ladled out a bowl of chili for Johnny Earth Tongue, grated some cheese onto it and took it out to the old man himself. He sat down next to him and pulled out his cigarettes. Grace had already cleaned up the mess and returned to setting the tables. Dottie was nowhere to be seen. Except for the whirring of overhead fans, the restaurant was perfectly quiet.

"What do you say, Johnny?" Harry lit up a smoke.

The Indian ate silently, as was his habit.

"That fella had an ugly disposition, I'll grant him that." Harry liked talking to Old Johnny. No matter what he said, he was never contradicted. The Indian managed to grunt an affirmation now and then, and he didn't eat too loudly.

"I guess he belongs to some biker gang. Call themselves the Ravens. Probably all come back here some time and trash the place. Hope it ain't on my shift. Maybe Bruce will be in here, might be he could sing 'em a song to quiet 'em down." Harry laughed at his own joke and looked over at Grace, but she was too busy to notice his lame attempt at humor. This was usually the time when Grace's company came in handy, between two and five, when the place was dead and there was nothing to do but clean up a little and prepare for the morning rush. Harry could see she wasn't in the mood for jokes tonight. When she was done, she went to the the back of the restaurant.

Dottie came out from the direction of the restrooms, her hair bobbed back into place and her makeup redone. After pausing to whisper something to Grace, she approached Harry and Johnny Earth Tongue. She had a pile of newspapers left behind by a customer, and dropped it down on the counter next to Harry's empty coffee cup. She went around the counter and brought the pot over, refilling first the Indian's, then Harry's, and her own cup.

"Tonight," Johnny murmured while finishing his meal, "is the night Raven steals the moon."

"Is that right?" Harry smiled at the Indian, who was always saying something odd like that. Harry never knew whether it was native poetry or just more boozey talk, but it usually pleased him to hear it and always made him wonder. "Are we talking about the same person? About this Raven fellow, I mean."

Johnny nodded gravely, wiping a bit of chili from the side of his mouth. "Yes. Raven made the sky and put the stars in their proper places."

"That's not the way I heard it, Johnny."

"It is so. I know all the stories. Tonight he steals the moon for awhile, but later on he will give it back."

Dottie rattled the paper and laughed to herself. Harry took a section of paper and lucked upon the comics. He read them silently between sips of coffee.

"Where's Grace?" Harry asked.

Dottie looked over at him, "She's mopping the bathrooms. I told her she didn't have to do that. I told her she was a waitress, not a janitor. She said she felt restless and needed to keep busy."

"I think I'll go check on her," Harry said.

At three in the morning the silence in the coffee shop was made up of sounds so familiar Harry no longer heard them; the buzz of the fans, the refrigerator hum, the imperceptible noise of fluorescent lighting. Beyond the glass doors, the desert was a fallen curtain revealing a window to the stars. Harry walked down the hallway leading to the restrooms.

Grace was sitting on the floor, her head resting at an angle against the white tiled wall, her hands folded in her lap. The mop and bucket had been pushed into a corner and left there. She didn't bother to look at Harry as he took a seat on the ceramic sink. Leaning back, his left shoulder rested uncomfortably against the soap dispenser, but he stayed where he was, not wanting to spook her. He looked at Grace and then looked down at his thick, ringless fingers. After a couple of minutes, he cleared his throat again, and spoke.

"Want to talk about it?" he asked quietly.

She did not answer him, but when she looked up Harry could see something frightening in her. She had always been a pretty girl, but now her eyes were haggard and her makeup streaked down her cheeks and a lost, vacant stare had replaced the bright sparkle that had always been her special redeeming charm. It seemed to Harry that she was aging right in front of him.

"Grace," he spoke again, "you can talk to me."

"I tried to tell Wayne about it before he left," said Grace, "but he was so busy getting his gear together."

"What were you going to tell him?" Harry asked.

"I'm pregnant, Harry."

Harry paused, then smiled, "Well, if I was Wayne I'd be tickled to death."

"Thanks, Harry . . . but if you were Wayne you'd probably figure out that we didn't make love last month. Not the month before that, either."

"Well," he sighed, "what're you gonna do?"

"He doesn't know what it's like for me here. I don't have any friends outside of work. Nobody to talk to. And if I did, what could we do out here in this damn town anyway? All anybody does around here is work, sleep, screw or get drunk."

"It's no kind of life," Harry agreed. He had never really pictured things that way, but he knew she was right about Solero. And he knew he would probably never leave.

The breakfast rush was light that morning. He wiped down the grill and removed spots of splattered grease from the adjacent walls. During the last half hour of his shift, Harry decided to take another break.

Standing between two big deisels in the parking lot, he watched the sky go from mauve to red to a bright pink-orange. The tall arms of the saguaros were trimmed with a fuzzy whiteness, and the moon hung like a dirty plate.

A sudden breeze came up and lifted his apron against his chest. As he turned to go back he saw something in the distance, a dark shape on the horizon. He shivered involuntarily. A flock of crows was approaching from the southeast. The closer they flew, the brighter the sky became. Soon they were so close he could hear them, one at a time, cawing to each other in harsh, mocking voices as the first glaring shafts of sunlight pounded into his eyes.

By the time Harry reached the kitchen entrance at the back of the coffee shop they had already passed overhead. As he opened the door, he looked up into the pale morning sky and noticed the crows circling something out beyond the highway. He couldn't see what it was, an animal in trouble probably, or fresh road kill thrown clear of the pavement. All he knew was that they were lowering in a tight pattern, gradually closing ground, each black bird waiting for its turn.

*R*oute 66 revived the town in the mid-1930s. Isolated halfway between Kingman and Barstow, Solero provided the Highway Department with the perfect location for a maintenance barracks. The road itself brought back jobs and money to that barren corner of nowhere. The need for roadside services created a string of diners, garages and motor courts at the western edge of town. Tourists passed through, took photographs of the river and the surrounding hills, then vanished in their big automobiles down the ribbons of freshly rolled asphalt.

In the years that followed, fortunes were made turning the surrounding wasteland into productive acres of cotton, lettuce and alfalfa. The soil was rich with alluvial deposits and flat green fields stretched uninterrupted from Blythe to Yuma. The Moabis did not lose sight of their ancestral calling. They were able to secure territorial rights over much of their historical lands, conceding certain right-of-ways to the Water and Highway Departments. In exchange, they received government loans and subsidies that enabled them to buy the heavy equipment needed for clearing, planting and harvesting the surrounding desert. The tribe prospered in the burgeoning agricultural industry.

# Under the River

Johnny Earth Tongue was walking home through the swamp, making his way with a willow staff and carrying over his shoulder a burlap sack. The trail was bordered on either side by an impenetrable wall of yellow tules. Beyond the tall reeds stood invisible graves of submerged cottonwoods, the tallest branches poking up like black bones through the glassy surface of the river.

The trail cut across the marshy sedges, a narrow track of white sand only slightly elevated above the high watermark. It was an ancient footpath, used by natives during times of prehistoric flooding and now once again after the river had been diverted during the construction of an interstate highway bridge downstream. It was not accessible by car, nor did it exist on any map.

Johnny was being followed at a distance of twenty feet by a large black dog. The dog was the kind used by hunters to retrieve downed waterfowl. Its long, quivering snout was tilted into the sunset breeze that blew off the sack. The thick barrel of its chest gasped for air, ribs heaving under stiff black fur, as if the exhausted animal had come a long way to get there.

They walked on for a mile or more, the old man leading the way with the dog not far behind. The sun was down and the western sky stretched out before them with high feathery streaks of pink and silver clouds. On the horizon, the Big Maria Mountains rose, one range after another, like dark swells on a lunar sea. Blacktailed swallows cut swiftly back and forth through the lowering dusk, easily catching gnats in the twilight.

Johnny noticed an awkward figure struggling out of the slough, up the shallow bank and onto the trail in front of him. The man wore rubber pants secured by suspenders, a thick wool jacket, and a bright orange hunting cap. He cradled a shotgun beneath his right arm. When the hunter had cleared the wet tules, he paused and stood rocking slightly at the very edge of the footpath, then staggered to the center of it. He turned abruptly and saw the old man coming slowly towards him, followed by the black retriever.

"There you are!" cried the hunter. "Where the hell have you been, you sonuvabitching hound dog? Heel, Hondo, heel!"

Even without seeing his face, Johnny recognized Jack Nooncaster from the Highway Department. He had heard the same voice often enough in the bars of Solero to recognize its owner out here in the middle of the swamp. He didn't want to stop and talk, but the path was blocked and he didn't see any way to avoid it. He thought of turning around and hurrying back deeper into the swamp, but it was too late for that.

"Goddam you to hell, Hondo, heel!"

The dog attempted to scurry past Johnny, but the trail was too narrow so it stopped short, giving ground and panting heavily with pink-flecked nostrils pointing straight at the sack. Its body shivered involuntarily and the dog began to whine as if in pain or nervous distress.

"Can you believe that stupid bastard?" Nooncaster loomed up out of the darkness, shaking his orange-capped head. "I paid five hundred dollars to have him trained and just look."

Johnny turned around to observe the dog for the first time. All the while the black shadow had followed him, he hadn't paid attention to it, but now he saw what a handsome creature it really was, a pelt of slick smooth fur stretched over long bones and rippling muscles, a knot of bone between the ears signifying its canine intelligence, and eyes like liquid gold.

Nooncaster brushed by him and approached the big retriever.

"I've been lookin' for you, Hondo. For three hours, I've been crawlin' through the muck. Now, heel, goddamit."

The dog cowered as Nooncaster came toward him, its whiplike tail pumping helplessly against the sand. When he was almost to the dog, Nooncaster stooped to pick a stick from the ground. While the lab sat obediently, the hunter raised the dry cottonwood branch as if he were about lash it down across the dog's head and, wheeling suddenly around, threw the stick far into the tangled reeds. Faltering for an instant, the dog let out a short, pitiful yelp and bounded off, thrashing into the marsh.

"Look at that, willya?" Nooncaster pointed at the spot where the retriever had disappeared.

Johnny didn't answer.

"Don't I know you?" Nooncaster walked back to where the old man stood. He raised the shotgun into full view, fumbling with his free hand in the inside pocket of his wool coat. "What's your name?"

"Earth Tongue."

"Sure, you're Ol' Johnny the Rattlesnake Man," Nooncaster finally pulled a pack of cigarettes from his chest pocket. "I'm a Johnny, too, but Jack to my friends."

He offered Johnny a cigarette. The Indian stared at the little white stick uncomprehendingly, shrugged his disinterest and resumed his slow, sure gait. Nooncaster hesitated, gazing back down the trail in the opposite direction as it quickly dissolved into the darkness a dozen yards away. He glanced toward the section of swamp where he had thrown the stick and where his dog splashed among the pointed shafts of recently submerged trees. Then he took a few long, fast strides and came up alongside Johnny. They walked on in silence, the old man with his staff and sack, the burly hunter with his shotgun and cigarette. Dark clouds were lowering into the valley from the south and the sunset subsided rapidly into a moonless, windy night.

"Rumor has it," Nooncaster exhaled smoke, "there are wild boars in this part of the swamp. A buddy of mine saw two of them yesterday up near Five Mile Landing. Perfect monsters, he told me, with tusks big around as your forearm."

"Uh," Johnny grunted, "Two."

"Monsters. Aggressive as hell, from what I hear."

"Not monsters," Johnny shook his head.

"What?"

"Old ones whose eyes look backwards."

Nooncaster laughed. "You Indians say the goddamndest things."

Johnny didn't respond, but he looked over to study the hunter's face. His eyes were adjusted to the dark, while Nooncaster glared weakly into the shadows. The hunter's day-old beard gave him a mean, hungry look, but his jowls were thick and bulky, with a sagging fold of skin beneath his chin. He scratched absently at his left ear as he walked. The rest of his body mirrored his facial expression, soft and fat and unaware of the things around him. In the crook of his right arm, the shotgun swung carelessly. Johnny wondered if it was loaded.

"This is the trail to the highway." Nooncaster looked around, unsure of himself. With the tules rising up all around it was impossible to see anything but the few feet of sand that appeared before them.

"You lost, mister?" Johnny asked.

"No, I'm not lost. I've hunted this swamp for years. Never been lost, not once. This is the trail back to the highway. I been on it many a night, and in worse shape than this, I'll have you know."

"Good," Johnny said.

"But it seems like there used to be a river in here." Nooncaster was still unsure. "This is where the old Mojave branched off the Colorado, ain't it? Before they dredged this swamp and made a friggin' lake out of the cottonwood groves."

"That sure right," Johnny nodded in the dark. "No more river here no more."

They had gone less than a mile before the dog caught up with them. It came loping up the trail from behind, the stick clamped tight between its powerful jaws. Its slick wet coat seemed even blacker in the dark. Nooncaster looked back at his retriever and laughed. The dog advanced closer with its ears up, but when it caught scent of the sack it stiffened, dropping the stick and falling back a safe distance from the two men. Long strings of saliva hung from its mouth.

"He sure is actin' funny," Nooncaster said. "Usually, he walks so close to me I have to knee him to keep from gettin' tripped. Wonder what's botherin' him."

Johnny Earth Tongue had no opinion on the matter. He moved with a minimum of effort, probing the ground in front of his feet with the staff. All he knew was that he had

walked for several hours and was not yet tired, and that, if
he had to, could walk for several more.

"Where the hell are we, anyway?" Nooncaster was
getting irritated with the taciturn old man. He had been
hunting in the marsh all day, had never even seen a duck,
and had finished off the last of his whiskey hours ago. He
had become separated from his dog a few hours before
sundown, and was completely lost when he accidentally
came across the trail and met up with Johnny and Hondo.
It was getting darker by the minute and the wind carried
an odor of rain.

"How much further to the highway?" he asked.

"Which highway?" Johnny wanted to know.

"Old 95. My car's parked off the side of the road near
Five Mile Landing."

"Johnny don't drive."

Nooncaster lit another cigarette. The brief illumination
of flame revealed an unfamiliar landscape, full of leafless,
contorted trees and wind-whipped reeds. He wiped at his
nose,and adjusted the collar of his coat around his neck.
He shifted the shotgun under the other arm. The reeds
made an incessant racket that bothered Nooncaster and
put him on edge.

"What you got in the bag, Johnny? Catch your dinner?"

"No."

"Well, what the hell is it? My dog's been actin' real
strange and I think it might have somethin' to do with
whatever you got in that bag."

"Your dog smarter than he look."

"Yeah? Did I tell you what I paid for the bastard? Bred
in a kennel in Upper Michigan . . ."

Something slow and heavy rattled through the reeds
nearby. Nooncaster jumped back and aimed the shotgun
towards the sudden noise. The dog who had been
roaming invisibly behind him surged forward with a
throaty growl. The tules shook for a moment and then

were quiet. Water could be heard lapping through the brittle stalks along the unseen shore. All was inky darkness with unaccountable night sounds coming from the direction of the missing river. The dog went over and sniffed the sand a few paces away. Johnny walked on quickly without looking to the right or left.

Nooncaster had to hurry to catch up with him. "Wait, hold on there!" He was breathing hard and his voice now was different than the one he used to hire and fire road workers back in the Buffalo Nickel Saloon.

"That sounded like a goddam wild boar! It wasn't more than ten yards away when it went into the water. Didn't you see it?"

"Yeah."

"What was it?"

"Don't know."

"You think it might be a boar?"

"Boar don't like water so much," Johnny said, "and don't like people at all."

"Shit! It ain't safe out here after dark, is it?"

Johnny didn't reply, but kept walking at a brisk pace. Nooncaster followed him, with the lab trailing a few yards behind. They walked on in that order for another mile or more, until Nooncaster began to lose his wind. He didn't want to stop, for fear the old man would leave him behind. By now he had begun to doubt his location in the swamp, and the Indian was his only chance of getting out that night. At the same time, he wasn't in shape to keep up. Finally, he took a few quick steps and came up beside Johnny.

"Can we stop for a minute, buddy?" Nooncaster reached for the old man, but his hand grabbed the sack instead. He immediately jerked his hand back, as if pricked by a cactus needle.

Johnny stopped walking, turned, and looked at the Highway Department foreman, whose face seemed contorted in the dark.

"Better we don't stop here," he whispered.

"Why the hell not?"

"Mastamaho," Johnny said.

"Who is that?"

Johnny glanced off towards the sound of water rippling, then grunted, "Old ones whose eyes look backwards."

"I heard you say that Indian crap before. I didn't get it then and I don't get it now! Talk straight, old man, or I'll bust your chops."

"Mastamaho," Johnny spoke in earnest. "The old ones. They live under the river."

Nooncaster forced himself to laugh.

"I go now," Johnny said.

"Wait a damn minute," Nooncaster was getting angry. "Where is the goddam highway and my car?"

"You said you not lost."

"You're goddam right I'm not lost." Nooncaster heard his own voice swallowed up in the rattling of the reeds nearby. Johnny turned away, as if to leave.

"Just a flippin' minute, Tonto!"

Nooncaster swung the shotgun up to his chest, the long straight barrel pointing directly at the old man's groin. Johnny paused. He could see the rage that locked the white man's face in anger.

"What is that you got in the bag?" Nooncaster shouted.

"My poison brothers," Johnny said.

"Like hell it is," said Nooncaster. "I want to see."

The two men were standing about five feet apart. Each could just make out the features of the other across the length of shadow between them. Johnny Earth Tongue smiled, a thin curving of his lips, weary and humorless. The burlap sack dropped from his grip between them, the top spread half-open at their feet. Nooncaster stood unmoving, the shotgun gripped in his hands. He looked down at the motionless brown folds with an expression of astonished disbelief. He suddenly felt exhausted.

"What are you doing?" he heard himself say.

"Letting you see him," Johnny answered.

"Who?" Nooncaster spoke quietly.

"Don't worry ," said Johnny, "He can't hear you. This is where we buried our people. Before you built that highway you can't find. Now they live under the river."

"Christalmighty," the hunter croaked, still unable to move.

The old man watched him curiously. All at once, the adrenaline coursing through Nooncaster's veins reached his brain and he jumped backwards. At the same time, the dog leaped forward and took a protective stance between the sack and his master. Nooncaster fumbled with the zipper of his jacket, until his fingers found their way to the inner lining. He found a shell and jammed it into the stock of the shotgun and snapped the gun back across his shoulder, this time pointing the barrel towards the ground at the Johnny's feet.

"You've had it!" he screamed. "Now, you're gonna tell me where the goddam highway is!"

Johnny bent down to pick up the burlap sack, much too carelessly, and tossed it like a bag of harmless squash across his back. He looked at the hunter curiously. The dog quit barking, but continued to whine in a sad, low pitch. He moved away from Nooncaster and the dog. Black was an unlucky color to be at night.

The hunter's mouth felt stuffed with cotton. He jerked his shotgun upright towards the Indian's back, aiming at the limp bundle of burlap swinging like a pendulum behind him. He held the stock against his shoulder for several seconds, until his arm ached and the old man was out of sight. Then he lowered it slowly and fished around in his pocket for another cigarette, his fingers shaking uncontrollably. It was then that he realized his hand was beginning to burn.

W hen plans for the new Interstate business loop were revealed, the citizens of Solero discovered that the highway bypassed the town by several miles. Now, instead of entering Solero as you might have expected, you skirted the original settlement without ever seeing the old downtown, driving instead past empty railheads and vacant homestead shacks and fields of junked automobiles, then off across a deep ravine on the new cement overpass.

The freeway exit officially bypassed Solero by 2.8 miles, a fact which became painfully obvious to its deceived and misrepresented inhabitants; the lonesome hamburger jacks, restless busboys, divorced waitresses, drunk mechanics, barren pump jocks, nostalgic tow truck drivers, lodeless miners, one-armed brakemen, and ex-rodeo stars in wheelchairs—Indians and Mexicans and Gringos alike—each man, woman and child reduced to a curiosity for passing strangers, like postcard images from a ghost town.

# Natives in Exile

It was going to rain. All afternoon the long, slow, grey clouds had sloped into the basin, above the river and west towards the hills. Old Highway 95 ran along the plane of the desert like a black thread of paint across a sanded floor. The new Interstate pierced the rhyolite mountains to the east and cut sharply south, converging with Route 66 at Top Rock. The old road back to Solero ran through the swamp, over a concrete bridge, and headlong into the belly of the storm.

Neat rows of palm trees stood along the last California exit, evenly spaced down the ramp to the frontage road below. A Highway Department pickup was parked in the shoulder gravel beside the road. Two nursery palms leaned from either end of the truck's scratched bed. The roots of the young plants were wrapped in burlap and the newly opened fronds were covered with a fine yellow hair, as if they had just been born.

Jose Pomona was working alongside the pickup, chipping away at the earth with a shovel and stopping

143

periodically to study the progress of the approaching storm. Another, smaller shovel and a pair of posthole diggers lay on the ground beside a dark pile of turned sand. The pile mounted as he knelt lower and lower to dig.

A shaft of sunlight lancing through the clouds pushed Jose's shadow over the asphalt behind him. After working tenaciously for several minutes, he finally dropped the shovel and stepped into the hole, knee-deep. Scooping the bottom with his hands, he cleared the hole and climbed back out.

Returning to the rear of the truck, Pomona took hold of one of the palms and slid it to the edge of the bed. With a pocket knife, he cut the twine that held the burlap around the roots. Then, avoiding the sharp new fronds that swung overhead, he rolled it off. The tree dropped hard, thudding on the packed gravel. Dirt caked between the roots was flung away, and the raw whitish skin lay exposed. He dragged it off the road shoulder and brought it up beside the shovel. Setting the plant upright, he lowered it carefully and started filling the hole.

Darkness came quickly with low clouds blotting out the crimson sunset. Mr. Willy Two Childs navigated the reservation road, peering ahead through his headlights at passing circles of asphalt and brush. Coyote Tom was crouched down in the seat beside him, asleep. Willy spoke to him anyway, carrying on an animated conversation. As he drove and spoke, Willy gestured vaguely at the distant lights of Solero blinking on ahead of them in the storm-hurried dusk.

". . . and we can't sleep in the house of your cousin, because her husband wants to shoot you. He still blames us for what happened that night over at the dance hall in Kingman. You remember. She took advantage of the situation. Besides, it may not rain at all. In that case, we

can sleep on the bed of the truck. I have an old paint tarp
that will keep us dry."

He glanced over at Coyote.

". . . and you can use it, my friend. Not that I'm scared
of your cousin's husband. I might just have to handle him
myself."

The flatbed rattled along, approaching the web of
lights with slow determination. Its tires edged just beyond
the blacktop, skidding on the gravel shoulder, but Willy
quickly swerved them back onto the highway. He grew
silent for awhile, concentrating on the task of driving. A
jackrabbit leaped from the roadside as he topped a small
hill, merging with the brush in a sudden clash of lamplight
and shadow. At that moment a bright flash of purple
encompassed the southern sky. Willy straightened up with
his long bony fingers clamped around the steering wheel.

". . . and what is a little lightning? The old ones say it
carries the power of Mastamaho, but I don't believe in
that evil spirit crap. Neither do you, Coyote. Am I right?
Maybe it is an omen . . . an omen that we should stay in
town tonight, not risk driving home in the rain. Don't you
think so? Once we have taken everyone's pool money over
at the Buffalo Nickel Saloon we should come back to my
truck and lie on the bed and watch the bright lights
flashing. That is a thing men should learn to do. You and I
will be warm enough with this in our blood."

Clasping the wheel with one hand, he reached the other
down between his legs and brought from under the seat a
black-labelled bottle. He unscrewed it by taking the cap
hard between his teeth and rotating the bottle with his free
hand until the neck came away from his mouth. Still
holding the cap with his teeth, he raised the whiskey and
drank sideways. He took the bottle away from his lips and
pushed the black cap with his tongue up under his cheek,
then let out a hoarse stuttering gasp. He blinked his eyes
tightly shut, then wide open, until they began to water.

The tires skidded again on the shoulder gravel. He stared watery-eyed through the dirty windshield, aiming the truck back into the lane. Coyote slept on beside him.

"A little rain," said Willy. "A little thunder. A little lightning in a bottle. Sure enough. Your cousin's husband better stay home tonight."

Out of the darkness ahead, a gas station appeared, its orange globe hanging motionless against the ominous horizon. A few miles beyond it, the blinking lights of the town appeared like a pit of fluttering coals. He capped the bottle, using again the well-developed motion between his free hand and his teeth. He slid it back under the seat and nudged his friend awake.

Coyote Tom unfolded slowly . His hair was pressed the wrong way over his face, and as he sat up he shook it back across his shoulders. It was long and black and tangled, the way a mop gets. His face was still puffy with sleep as the truck passed under the first streetlamps on the northern edge of town. He rubbed at his eyes and grunted, saying nothing as Willy prattled on.

"Have you ever noticed how neon draws women into town, like moths to a yardlamp? Sizzle and zap! That's what'll happen when they bump into us."

Coyote mumbled a series of obscenities and tried to direct the aimless pattern of his hair. He was already hungover from an afternoon of drinking back at the reservation pool hall. His mouth tasted of ashes and his tongue was numb. His eyes shrank to slits as they passed oncoming traffic. Finally seated erect, he leaned over the dash to see exactly where they were. The truck rounded a lamplit corner and headed down Main. At the end of the street, two rows of buildings faced each other across a black expanse of asphalt, with several cars and pickups parked in slanted spaces on either side.

"Have some more of the dog's hair," said Willy. He had the bottle open again and was handing it to Coyote. "Take a good long swallow to get your blood moving."

Coyote tipped up the bottle and chugged the whiskey. He brought it down and wiped his mouth on the back of his sleeve. Then he handed it back, gravely silent, as Willy swung the truck with one hand into a vacant lot beside a square brick building and cut the engine. He, too, took a last, long drink.

A jagged white bolt struck just beyond the ring of lights. The ensuing rumble seemed to erupt from the throat of the earth. Across the street, in the garret window above the abandoned laundromat, a lamp sparked and faltered but regained its thin glow. The silhouette of a man's upper body rested in one corner, a high-crowned cowboy hat upon his head. Mr. Willy Two Childs drained the bottle and tossed it out of the truck. The glass shattered in the empty lot. Willy let out a whoop and whistled, shaking his head as if something were loose inside. Then he turned to Coyote, who was slumped against the opposite door, rubbing at his forehead and irritably rearranging his snarled hair.

"I'm broke," he said. "Don't you have any money left?"

"No," said Coyote, "just the coin."

A battered station wagon pulled up under the row of flashing signs advertising the barrooms, pool halls and massage parlors of Solero, and halted with the engine running. For a moment shadowy figures stirred inside and then the passenger door swung open over the curb. Two boys climbed out of the station wagon, the second reluctantly drawn by the first, both bundled in yellow raincoats and hats. The first boy, the smaller of the two, leaned back in to speak with his mother.

"You can stay with Uncle Harry," said Dottie Smith. As she spoke to her youngest son she checked her makeup in the rearview mirror. "He told me he would look after you if I ever needed a sitter in a pinch . . . and that's what this is, a pinch. Are you listening, hon'?"

The boy wiped his nose with the back of his hand and nodded.

"I'll be at the Top Rock Marina if he needs to call me. Tell Harry I will be by his house to pick you up before midnight. Can you tell him for me, sweets?"

"It's gonna rain, mama," the boy looked up into the close, starless sky. "Gonna rain a hard one tonight, I think."

"It just might. You keep your brother dry. Harry will be in one of these buildings, probably right in there. I see his car parked across the street. Here's a dollar to buy you some Cokes." Dottie reached for the boy and puckered her glossy red lips. "Give mama a kiss. You boys be good."

The boy kissed his mother as she handed him the money. Then he stepped back and she slammed the door shut. The station wagon pulled abruptly away from the curb, quickly moving down the street, beyond the lights, and off into the velvet darkness. The two boys stood close together on the pavement, staring at the red taillights as they grew smaller, became pinpoints and finally disappeared.

Taking the larger boy by the hand, the younger brother, whose name was Bobby, turned and began walking slowly along the sidewalk, pausing every few steps to peer through a dusty window or listen to the voices escaping out a half-open door. When they reached the end of the block, they stopped for a moment, turned around, then retraced their steps methodically until they reached the opposite corner. Once there, Bobby motioned for his brother, Frank, to sit down. Frank instantly obeyed. He sat at the curb and began to play with the sand and pebbles that lay between his feet in the gutter. Hands in pockets, Bobby remained standing and watched in silence the low reel of neon blinking in windows and over doors all down the block.

"Mama said to find Uncle Harry," Bobby said to himself. "She said to keep you dry and drink Cokes until she come to get us. She's coming back at midnight. We have to be to Uncle Harry's at midnight."

Frank made a gurgling noise and held up some pebbles for Bobby to see.

"They's pretty rocks, ain't they?" Bobby nodded.

From the west, somewhere out in the desert, came a distant sound. Bobby looked down at his sneakers and listened for the long sustained note to end. It did, and soon came again, a little closer this time. He looked up when it was over and stared towards the blank wall of darkness encircling the town. The boy on the curb looked up too, and swiveled towards his brother. It was a sound he knew. His round eyes swept the horizon in anticipation.

"You hear it, don't you?" Bobby said. He brought his hands up out of his raincoat and rubbed them together. It was getting colder, and a wind had begun to pick up around them. Frank raised his cupped hands to his mouth and curled his lips into an "O," sending white puffs of steam into the chilly air.

"Yeah," Bobby smiled, "the train is coming. How many cars you think this one is pullin'?"

He peered into the darkness, listening hard for the sound to come again. It did not return. This confused him. He looked back at his brother, who had become transfixed by the traffic lights overhead. A box above them flipped from red to green. In the crosswalk, two men appeared, approaching them with the loud clop of their boots on blacktop. The pair emerged like phantoms, encrimsoned with light from the signals. Half the way across Bobby could see them clearly. He quickly bent down and took Frank by the arm. The brothers shuffled into the shadows beyond the lamplight and stopped, leaning against the brick facade of the first building on the block. They watched the phantoms pass from there.

"Indians," whispered Bobby. He could feel Frank's warm breath against the nape of his neck as the older boy stared over his shoulder warily. When the Indians were past, the brothers edged forward to the very corner of the building. With necks outstretched, they watched the Indians hesitate outside one of the bars, then push through the heavy wooden door, the one left slightly ajar to allow the smoke and laughter and music to seep out onto the sidewalk and hang there, ghostlike, before blowing away on the gusty wind.

The air in the Buffalo Nickel was rank. The smell of cigar smoke made Coyote's stomach clench. He pushed a strand of hair out of his eyes and squinted, following the sound of Two Child's banter to an empty table near the bar. Willy was waving and calling out names, but nobody seemed to answer. Coyote crumbled into his chair and remained motionless, trying to fight the feeling that his feet were floating up over his head. With eyes cracked open, he glared around the smoky room.

The easiest figure to discern was a fat balding man stretched over a pool table, taking long deliberate test strokes with his cue over a bandaged hand. His shining scalp glowed pink under the table lamp. The red cherry of a cigar butt protruded from the side of his mouth. Half a dozen faces were hazily outlined against the panelled wall, watching the bald man at work. Back in the far corner, a purple jukebox throbbed its warm light against the ceiling, all the sounds and voices in the bar underlined by the sad whine of a pedal steel guitar.

Willy, who had momentarily disappeared, suddenly stood before him, shaking his head and frowning. "Just like I thought . . . our credit is shot. They showed me the tab. You never told me you broke a chair in here last month."

Coyote didn't feel like talking. The nausea had risen up to a place just under his lungs, and he thought that if he opened his mouth everything he had swallowed that afternoon would come pouring out.

"Looks like we gotta hawk the coin. You do have it on you now, don't you?"

Coyote said nothing. The smoke was coating his mouth and tongue and he needed something to wash it away. He sat up and took from the pocket of his shirt a small pouch made of deer leather. A single feather attached to the loop of string held it shut. He loosened the string and tipped the pouch over the table. A dull yellow coin clattered against the wood. Willy picked it up and turned it over in his palm. Coyote stared beyond him, the sickness beginning to tickle at the base of his throat.

"This is only to get us into a game. I'll win it back along with some cash and pretty soon we have what we need to make a run on the house across the street at BUD'S."

Coyote looked past him, not listening, not even hearing, his vision a long tunnel through which he could see the jowly bald man take slow deliberate aim and strike. The cue ball spanked into a nest of colored balls and one of them disappeared into a hole in the corner. The white ball came to rest directly below the hanging lamp. The other balls, scattered over the length of the table, cast small oval shadows away from it. The bald man took the cigar from his mouth and began to circle his next shot, bending over and cocking his head at eye level to the green plane. He stood up, scratched at his chin, hoisted his trousers, dusted his cue, and assumed position—head low, chin to shoulder, brows furrowed, his thick hairy arms extended in opposite directions. The stick slid back and forth over the bandaged hand, wiggling a little until he brought it back and held it, poised like an arrow in the perfect fusion of tension and calm. Then Coyote and the fat man and everyone else in the bar heard Willy's voice shouting above the din.

"Twenty-five? Are you crazy?" he cried, "Are you out of your gourd, Gordo?" He was standing at the bar thrusting the coin into the face of the bartender. "Twenty-five. . .you can't mean it. . .twenty-five bucks is all this is worth in here?"

The bald man stood up, exhaling a greyish mass of smoke. He looked hard towards the bar where Willy was standing with his back to the game.

"Victor," he croaked out of the side of his mouth, "who is that noisy bastard and why is he in here?"

"Sorry, Mr. Nooncaster, I'll see that he leaves right away." Victor dried his hands with a towel and looked menacingly at Willy.

"Good!" Nooncaster had the kind of voice that carried long distances without effort, delivering its message with intonation more than words. Coyote watched him turn back to the pool table, then stop and listen as Willy's voice rose even higher above the milling sounds of the bar.

"Gold!" he yelled. "A coin from the Spaniard's treasure." Victor had him by the collar now and was moving him towards the door, when Willy wriggled free and plunged towards the pool table.

"Hey!" Victor shouted, following Willy with a thick-fisted punch to the back. Willy stumbled towards the pool table, holding the coin tightly in his right hand as his left caught a chairback to keep him from falling over on his face.

"Ease up," commanded Nooncaster, and Victor stopped in his tracks. He left the Indian gripping the chair and returned to the bar. Everyone was silent, watching Nooncaster and Willy face each other across the lighted pool table. Willy smiled weakly and nodded in thanks to the foreman, whose bulging fists were gripping his pool cue like a club. Nooncaster's wide mouth worked furiously around the cigar, puffing and chewing and moving it side to side, until his face was obscured in a haze of smoke.

"So," Nooncaster said, "what is all this noise about a coin?"

"We have a piece of gold from the old Spanish treasure. We don't want to sell it, just trade it in on a game or two. After we win, we will settle up with the bar and get the coin back."

"Let me see that coin, buddy."

Willy brought the coin up right to his face, ignoring his outstretched hand. "Just look."

Nooncaster studied the coin in the same way he would study his next shot. He leaned across the table, tilting his head and appraising it with the same shifting of the eyes, the same interior calculation he used on his bank shots. He backed off, rubbing his chin, hoisting his pants, fastening his stare first on the coin, then on Willy. He scooped up a cube of blue chalk and began to dust the tip of his cue. Then he glanced back at the coin once more and smiled, exposing a set of crooked yellow teeth.

"That's quite a little gold piece you got there, buddy." He returned his attention to the pool table. "Yessir. . .quite a piece." Now everyone was looking towards the coin, glinting between Willy's upheld fingers. The room pulsed with purple jukebox light. Coyote needed a drink more than ever. Willy closed his hand around the coin in confirmation as Nooncaster continued.

"I'd say two, maybe, two-fifty is what you could ask for—on the open market, I mean. This ain't exactly the gold exchange on Wall Street, but I have to admit, it's worth two-fifty if it's worth a dime. Sure is."

"Alright, alright." This was Victor. "I'll set you up to a game with Jack. You win and tab is cleared. You lose and the coin is mine."

Willy glanced at Coyote, then turned back to the bar. "Two hundred dollars, take it or leave it."

"What?" The bartender was astonished.

"You heard me."

"Wait a second," said Victor, visibly angry. "You owe me seventy-three dollars. Pay up before you come in here looking to float a game of pool."

"I only want a fair bet," Willy said. "This coin is worth more than a clear tab and you know it."

"Get out!" Victor began wiping his hands again, ready to heave Willy through the door.

"Okay, I will, don't worry . . . somebody in this town knows a good deal when they see one." Willy approached the pool table one more time. "Maybe you wanna bet on this here coin, Jack, bein' as you're the only one in here who seems to know what it's worth."

Nooncaster did not bother to look up from the game. "No way, red man. You can pour all the Spaniard's treasure you got right here on this table and I wouldn't trade you a plugged nickel for it."

"No?"

"Hell, no!" boomed Nooncaster. "I told you before this ain't no gold exchange, and, besides, who's to say it's yours to sell? Maybe you just stole it off a drunk miner or worse. Maybe you bushwhacked the poor s.o.b. somewhere out there in the desert, left him buried under a rock and made off with his find, claimin' it all to yourself like the greedy bastard you appear to be. Coins like that gotta be registered with the authorities. You got the papers to go with your claim to that little piece? How about it, buddy?"

The other men in the bar glared suspiciously at Willy, muttering among themselves.

"Anybody seen ol' Ashpram lately?" one of them asked.

"I ain't seen him in three months," somebody answered.

"Where'd you come by that coin, red man?" asked Nooncaster.

"It belongs to Coyote Tom," said Willy, unconcerned by the brewing hostility in the crowded bar. "It was given to him by his grandfather, James Walking Bird, who dug it up down in Center Wash some thirty years ago. And Coyote's got the map shows just where the old guy found it."

All eyes followed Willy's pointing finger to where Coyote sat, face burrowed into his folded arms on the table. He could hear the voices buzzing all around him, making sounds he could not understand, tickling at his ear drums like bothersome gnats. Then came a shout and crashing of chairs and he thought he heard Willy Two Childs calling his name down a deep well, but the quiet was growing too fast to listen, and soon the dark fell warm around his shoulders.

The boys ran across the street when they saw the fight start. They charged into the VFW, halting just inside the door. They stood in a tiny vestibule with a small wooden table and on the table a ledger. The ledger lay open with a pen beside it and a small plaque which read PLEASE SIGN IN. The pages were covered with signatures. The vestibule lamp glowed a dim yellow. The two boys stared at the book. The little room opened onto a barroom on one side and a meeting hall on the other. They could hear the sound of a television coming from the bar. Bobby reached up and signed them both into the ledger. Then they went into the meeting hall.

The hall was empty. Rows of metal folding chairs sat open and unoccupied, facing a wooden podium at the far end of the room. Several flags hung on staffs planted in holders on either side of the podium. The walls were bare behind the podium, except for two small square windows and a framed portrait of Richard Nixon. On the walls to

either side of the folding chairs hung black and white
photographs of the town's war dead. Under each picture
was a typed label giving the soldier's name, birthdate, and
circumstance of death. The two boys walked slowly along
one of these walls, Bobby holding the hand of his older
brother, and reading each of the labels.

The two boys circled the room slowly, as if they were in
a museum, gazing intently at the thirty or so pictures on
the walls, each soldier's face staring back at them from
unsmiling faces and reflectionless eyes. Then they walked
back through the vestibule to the bar.

Two men were straddling stools at the bar counter.
Bobby recognized his Uncle Harry, but he didn't know
the other man. He towed Frank into the grimy yellow light
of the bar.

"Is that you, Bobby?" Harry was holding a mug of beer
to his mouth as he spoke.

"Hi, Uncle Harry." Bobby grinned.

"Well, well, and where is you boys' mama?"

Bobby brought Frank around so the the two men could
see him better. "She said you would have a Coke for
Frank. She said I could stay with you 'til she came home
from the dance over at the Marina tonight."

Harry's friend laughed into his beer while Harry
frowned and shook his head.

"Dottie has got you hooked," Harry's friend gurgled,
wiping the excess beer from his lips. "She sent the babies
after their sitter without tellin' you about it? What a move!
Oh, my stars, Harry, but you are nailed tonight."

"Shut up, Emmet Ray," Harry said. He smiled weakly at
Bobby and Frank, then dug down into his pocket for
some change. He fished out a quarter and some dimes and
handed them to Bobby. "Here you go, son. You and your
brother pick some music on the jukebox over there.
Anything you want to hear. It's alright with me."

"No rock'n'roll!" warned Emmet Ray.

"Thanks, Uncle Harry," Bobby smiled politely at the money in his hand and led his brother to the jukebox. The machine was planted in a dark corner, away from the bar. The two boys studied the song labels. Some were neatly typed and others were handwritten. Bobby deciphered one or two for Frank, who quickly lost interest. He only wanted to feed the coins into the slot and watch the lights throb with color once the music started. Bobby handed him a quarter. He smiled and launched it eagerly through the slot. Bobby made the selections and the first disk came off the rack.

"God, but I love Dean Martin," said Emmet Ray. He began to sing along with the record, "Goin' back to Houston . . . Houston."

"Come here, boys," said Uncle Harry, "and I'll buy you a Coke."

A television hummed above the bar. The bartender was adjusting the channel, but the picture did not improve. Race cars shot across the screen, their engines droning like locusts as the picture faded in and out.

"Can't you get that any better, Eddie?" asked Emmet Ray.

The bartender, who had been standing on a stool to reach the dials, stepped down and glared at Emmet Ray.

"Do it yourself, Ford. You're good with your hands, ain't you?"

Emmet Ray's eyebrows collided over his nose, knotting up into ridges of grey and black, and the scars on his forehead stood out in a pulsing rage. "Let's go, Harry. We'll take our business over to BUD'S. He don't make you kiss his feet every time he serves up a beer."

"Now, Emmet Ray, hold on," Harry was trying to calm his friend, but it was too late. Emmet Ray Ford was already headed towards the door in the vestibule.

"Sorry about that, Eddie," Harry apologized.

"Don't worry, I know all about that man's moodiness. He'll be singing love songs again in about fifteen minutes if he can get another beer down his throat without choking on his gall."

"Come on, boys." Harry motioned for Bobby and Frank to follow. "Your Uncle Harry is headed across the street. I guess you gotta stick with me, at least 'til your dancin' mama gets back."

"What about the music, Uncle Harry? I punched three songs and the first one isn't over yet."

"That's okay. It's paid for. They got a fancier box across the street at BUD'S. You'll like it there. I believe they even got a pinball machine."

"But Uncle Harry, wait . . ." Bobby held his brother close to him and looked towards the door.

"Yeah, Bobby, what's the matter?"

"There's Indians out there, Uncle Harry."

Coyote was shaken awake. The stench of vomit made him gag, and he lifted his head away from it. He felt something like anger at being shoved awake, but he did not know who to be angry with. Blue lamps shined around him and he heard his name being called again and again. The room was spinning in darkness, and angry voices were behind and above and beside him, and his own anger suddenly turned to fear. He thought he saw the face of Willy Two Childs, grimacing as if in pain, and then there was a stab of light exploding at a point behind his left ear. When the ceiling looped over to become the floor, all the voices ceased except for one.

"Coyote, do you hear me?" asked Willy. His head was obscured by clouds and his hands reached down from a great distance to right the slumping Coyote. Coyote's eyes glimpsed the bending street and a long belt of lights along the horizon. He was cold now and the air cut into his lungs sharp and clean. He felt his buttocks flat against the pavement and saw his boots in the gutter. He dropped his head between his knees and wretched.

"Are you alright?" Willy wanted to know. "That fat bastard hit you when you weren't lookin', right across your ear with his pool cue. I woulda clobbered him for you, only that greaseball Victor pulled some dirt on me, too."

Coyote pawed at his burning ear.

"Well, I tell you what . . . you listening to me, Coyote? We'll get even with those bastards. We'll make them wish they never crossed us. I swear to God, they will."

"The coin," Coyote gasped. He was ready to be sick again.

"Don't worry, I still got it. They couldn't pried it outta my grip with a cat's claw hammer."

Coyote coughed up a bitter liquid.

"Lightning in a bottle," Willy said. His friend was a dark figure of convulsion beneath the streetlamp, spitting strings of saliva to the ground. Willy stood over him, looming into the sky, the coin clenched tightly in his fist. Coyote pushed a strand of hair back around his good ear. He shivered with cold. A pool of yellow vomit was steaming between his feet. He wiped at his mouth and, shielding his eyes from the streetlight, peered up at Willy. He spoke, his voice as hollow and rough as raked gravel.

"I don't want to sell it. I want to keep my grandfather's gold."

Willy looked down at him. "The coin is yours. You can do whatever you want with it." He held the coin up to the light, admiring the smooth gravure of its surface.

"I want to throw it in the river. Then come back here and tell Nooncaster where it is."

"That's a good one, Coyote, real good." Willy was smiling. "I'd like to be there for that."

"You will be."

"Here's the coin."

"No, you keep it. It's heavy . . . and I feel weak tonight."

"Let's get out of the wet. This ain't the only place in town where a man can barter for a drink."

Coyote nodded his bowed head. He felt his legs moving, but it was as if they had gotten up without him. The strange sense of dislocation stayed with him as they walked down the block.

"I've been to war and back," said Coyote.

"Damn right you have!" Willy pounded his boots against the pavement. "They can't treat a good soldier like this, can they?"

Two successive flashes lit the clouded sky. A low groan of thunder rolled over the town, and a second stronger clap came slamming behind it. The thunder rolled on for several seconds and, lightly at first, it began to rain.

Working in the dark, Jose Pomona did not feel the first quick drops. He only noticed that the earth around the palm trees looked strangely spotted, and the blacktop appeared to be paved with diamonds in the direction of Solero. Under his zippered jacket, his pumping arms and chest grew steadily hotter. Then he could feel it raining.

Raindrops beaded on his face and hands while he worked. The last palm was planted and the moist topsoil fell from the shovel to the hole around it in thick clots. He stamped at the ground with his work boots, packing sand at the base of each young tree. He knelt to prop the drooping limbs of the first palm which had been damaged coming off the truck. The rain slanted down harder.

When he was done, Pomona stood up, grabbed his tools, and hurried back to the Highway Department pickup parked on the shoulder of the offramp. He tossed the tools in the bed of the truck and swung himself up into the cab, out of the galloping rain.

Searching the dashboard in darkness, he found a pack of cigarettes and a lighter. The rain washed hard and steady on the windshield, distorting the lights of town into bright streams of color across the glass. He lit a cigarette and inhaled, holding in the smoke for a moment. The sound of the rain increased, clattering on the roof and hood of the truck. He exhaled a small cloud of smoke which hovered over the steering wheel and slowly floated upward to spread along the ceiling of the cab. The windows began to fog over. He could smell the rain now, through the smoke, like the gnawing odor of rust on old metal.

A car went swishing by on the freeway headed east towards the bridge into Arizona. Pomona watched the red taillights diminish in the rainy distance as he finished his cigarette. He turned on the radio, hoping to catch the last of Brother Gabriel's Saturday evening broadcast. It came in scratchy and distant, so he had to strain to hear, but he soon recognized the message had something to do with Armageddon. He listened for awhile, smoking and watching the water wash in fine rivulets down the front of the truck's windshield.

Pomona stubbed the butt into the open ashtray and twisted the key in the ignition. The engine sputtered, bucked and cut out. He tried again, toeing the gas pedal delicately, careful not to choke it. The truck came to life with a throaty roar and he gunned the engine hard. The other smells in the cab were replaced by the reek of gasoline. As he levered the gears and pointed the truck back onto the frontage road, his headlamps fell across the two palms he had just planted. They stood like weary hitchhikers, listless and inert beside the Interstate off-ramp, bowed down under a sudden gust of wind.

Willy and Coyote were sitting on the pavement in the rain. They sat juxtaposed, chins to knees, backs hunched,

heads bowed to the silver street. The oilcloth jackets on
their backs were soaked dark brown. They sat like identi-
cal mounds of mud beneath the streetlamps, glistening.
The rain slackened. A car came down Main, its tires
hissing on the wet asphalt. At the intersection it stopped,
the yellow glow of the street suddenly becoming red. The
exhaust pipes huffed white clouds from the rear of the car.
The corner stoplight gleamed in the gutter where water
was pooling up in tiny red lakes over a clogged storm
drain. Then the tiny red lakes turned green and the car,
which had no muffler, growled down the street, still
audible long after it had passed from sight.

"Coyote," said Willy Two Childs.

"Uhm," his friend grunted.

"What we gonna do now?"

Coyote coughed and doubled over, his head hidden
between his knees.

"You okay?"

No answer.

"We shouldn't let those bastards in the Buffalo Nickel
throw us out on our butts."

The angry sound of motorcycles could be heard
through the drizzle, unwinding somewhere out on the
interstate.

"What did you say before?" Coyote asked without
looking up.

"I don't remember. What?"

"About lightening . . . and omens."

"That's what the old people think. Not me. I don't
believe all those crazy stories Johnny Earth Tongue likes
to tell when he's drunk."

Across the street, the door of the VFW swung open and
two men came out, followed closely by two boys. The
Indians watched them cross the street and enter another
bar. This one had a sign above the door which alternated
its message in red, white and blue neon: BUD'S (Beer and

Wine) . . . reflecting off the oilslick asphalt and haunting the vacant windows of the abandoned laundromat.

"Ain't that Emmet Ray Ford just went into that bar?" Willy sat up and rubbed his wet hands together.

"So?" mumbled Coyote.

"He has that station out on Old 95. You know the one."

"Yuh."

"We can offer him work for the price of a few beers. That would be better than hocking the coin."

"No." Coyote leaned sideways and coughed violently.

"Are you sick, Coyote?"

"No." The rain dripped off his black tangles to the gutter.

"Are you drunk?"

"No."

"Did that smack on the ear get you?"

"No."

"What's wrong?"

"When I got hurt in the war . . . the doctors, they left something inside me . . . something sharp."

Willy looked over at his friend. Coyote's face was buried in the folds of his coat and the water streamed down his shoulders and arms.

"You oughta talk to John Henry Flambeau about it. Maybe you can sue those bastards and retire."

Coyote looked up and smiled for the first time that evening. The lamplight gleamed on his hunched back. He put his arms out and rolled over on his side, then brought his knees down and turned completely over so he was lying flat on his stomach with his head towards the street. He made a yelping sound, like a dog being punished. His chin dropped over the curb of the pavement. And then, with his face in the gutter, Coyote muzzled water from the street.

"It's coming down pretty hard," Willy said. "I sure hope you don't drown!"

Coyote made a comical lapping noise.

"Hey, everyone," shouted Willy Two Childs, "come see the coyote drinking rain out of the gutter. I should shoot him and sell his skin to Jack Nooncaster. You know how much he hates coyotes."

Coyote sat up, grinning, and ran the back of his hand across his face in an exaggerated motion.

"Man, was I thirsty," he said.

The station wagon quit before it reached the bridge. Dottie could see the string of blue vapor lights tapering across the river and, beyond that, the white lamps from the marina shining weakly on the Arizona shore. She guided the car off the freeway onto the sandy shoulder and tried waggling the key to get it going again. The engine made a high whinnying noise, but refused to start.

"No!" pleaded Dottie, as if the ticking metal under the hood could hear and understand her wishes. "Not here, for godsakes, not now. Start!"

But it was no use. The engine was dead, probably for good. Every red light on the dashboard was lit up. The rain came down in short bursts, with long drizzly lulls in between. She removed her high heels and stuffed them into her purse, pulled the collar of her raincoat up around her neck, and made for the marina on foot.

It was raining hard. She didn't remember the desert ever raining like this—even in winter. She wrapped her arms tight around herself, clutching her coat closed to keep out the wind. It was about a half mile to the bridge, and several hundred yards further down a gravel slope to the marina. As she walked, she thought of her sons back in Solero. Bobby was young, only nine years old, but he had been looking after his older brother for several years and she trusted him to keep them both out of trouble. She wondered what the three of them were doing together, Bobby and Harry and Frank. Poor bewildered Frank.

Poor Harry, for that matter. He didn't get to have much fun, and the one night of the week he was allowed to seek it, she pulled a dirty trick like this on him. She would hear about it, come tomorrow night at work. But she knew how to handle Harry.

Dottie had reached the bridge and was just starting over it when she heard some kind of vehicle approaching in the distance. She could tell from the loud growling noise that it was a motorcycle. For some reason, this made her frightened for the first time since the station wagon quit. It was coming loud and fast and she could not cross the bridge before it arrived. There was nowhere to hide out on the bald span of concrete. Under the revealing glare of the vapor lights, she was completely exposed. She started to turn back, intending to step down off the Interstate and crouch low in a ditch. Then she turned and saw the lights coming.

"Harry!" she said, but nobody heard her.

The approaching headlights passed the last California exit at high speed. Dottie stood under the bridge lights, facing west. The highbeams played havoc with her eyes, but she refused to flinch and stared hard into the oncoming traffic.

They were past her in an instant. When the last one tore by, she was almost relieved, but she heard the engines throttle down half way across the bridge. Then she heard the first howl and her heart pushed out against the wall of her chest. It was a gang of bikers. They had stopped near the Arizona side of the bridge and were turning back, one by one. She wanted to scream, maybe alert someone over at the marina, but her throat felt somehow constricted and she knew her voice would never carry that far in the rain. She felt her hands gripping the cold steel railing and found herself looking down into the riverine darkness. She thought of jumping, but she was two hundred feet above the water and couldn't swim that well. Then she heard the first growling voice.

"Come to Papa!"

All the motorcycles had doubled back and were now pointing west on the eastbound lanes of the Interstate bridge, their engines alternately revving and downsurging, like racers at a starting line. She mentally pictured a semi barrelling across the stateline and knocking the bikes like so many bowling pins into the flowing black eternity below. But there wasn't another vehicle in sight for miles in either direction. Their lights were all trained on Dottie, the way floodlights used to adore starlets arriving for Hollywood premieres. Dottie suppressed once more the urge to jump, and turned to face them with a scowl on her face.

"What's your name, mama?"

"None of your business," Dottie hissed.

Hoots and howls and the hot steaming throb of idling engines surrounded Dottie. They straddled their bikes, legs akimbo, black leather gleaming in the weakening rain. She couldn't see their faces because of the lights, and had to shield her own from the piercing glare.

"What the hell are you doing out here?" This was the first question that seemed to include an inch of caring in it. She tried to look into the group of them, seeking the speaker, whose voice was oddly familiar.

"I'm walking, that's all," she finally answered.

"Walking, huh?"

"Yes, you ever heard of it? Real simple. One foot in front of the other. To get from A to B." Dottie's tongue had a tendency to get her in trouble, but it could also work to her advantage. She sensed the group was already amused by her, and had become less of a threat by virtue of that amusement.

"Well, kiss my tailpipe. If it isn't the busty little waitress from Sambo's." He turned to the others. "She's the one I

told you about who dropped a cold salad in my lap just to
be cute."

Dottie recognized his voice first, only because his face
was so difficult to see. It was the Chain, and this time he
was with the Ravens. She felt a dryness in her throat,
despite the rain.

"Let's take her," somebody croaked.

"Yeah, rescue the poor thing before she falls off the
bridge and drowns."

"We're on our way to Bullhead City," the Chain told her.
"You should come with us. It'll be a blast."

Dottie shivered, more from the cold than her fear.

"I can't ride on that." Her voice was hollow and without
conviction.

"Why not? You'd rather walk?"

"I'm already soaking wet. I'd probably turn to mud if I
rode a motorcycle all the way to Bullhead City without a
jacket on."

The Chain didn't hesitate. He pulled off his black
leather jacket and offered it towards her. Dottie thought
she could see the steam rising off his back. The inside of
the jacket was warm and lined with fur. At that moment,
the western sky flashed green with jagged brilliance. The
thunder came close behind, shaking through the ground
and into her bones. She thought of her two sons back in
town, of what their lives would be suddenly like without
her, of what her life would be like without them. Something was crystallizing inside her, like a fine crust of ice
around her heart, and it made her feel cold and lonely and
deeply in need. It was a foreign feeling, yet oddly familiar, like the chills during a fever, or deja vu. She put the
jacket on.

"What's it gonna be, sweetness? I'm willing to forgive
and forget. How about you?"

The Ravens balanced their bikes on the highway, their
boot heels on concrete, each poised with an amazing

surge of power at his fingertips, waiting for Dottie to
make up her mind.

   Bobby and Frank were in a phone booth on the corner
of Columbus and Main, across the street from BUD'S
(Beer and Wine). The rain hummed evenly on the glass,
and Frank was weeping quietly. Bobby was staring across
the street at the two dripping figures, sitting on the curb
with their boots in the gutter. He chewed at his upper lip in
silence, studying them. The two Indians appeared frozen,
trapped, unable to move away from the door of the bar.
From beyond the ring of lights which was the town's
northern edge came a distant moaning, gaining in volume
as it gathered speed. Frank cowered into one corner of the
booth.
   "Don't be scared," said Bobby. "It's just that train we
heard comin' before, only now it's goin' away. Hear it?"
   The dumb boy looked up at his brother with round
frightened eyes.
   "I gotta call the marina and talk to mama. Uncle Harry
told me to, so don't cry, okay?"
   A car rounded the corner and sped past them. It disappeared quickly in the rain, dissolving like an image on a
screen, beyond the feeble lamps and broken rays of
watery neon.
   "It's leaving the station. Gonna go right outta town to
Arizona. Mama's in Arizona, too."
   They were shivering in the booth. Huddled together,
they both pressed their faces against the glass and
watched the fogging pane go grey. They could hear the
train picking up steam. Down the street a railroad signal
began to clang. Red warning lights glinted on and off and
a long aluminum arm lowered on either side of the track.
Frank whimpered and clung to his brother, confused by
the sudden oscillation of lights and the doleful clanging of
the crossing bell. The booth was vibrating, they could

each feel it. Then the train emerged out of the darkness, glaring its fearsome white eye. The smoking engine bellowed long and loud. The heavy wheels rolling on the tracks made a steady clacking sound, counting off the ties. For a long time the freight cars passed, one after the other in hypnotic monotony. Bobby felt his brother's chin digging into his shoulder as the older boy nodded into a fitful half-sleep. He felt the final blast of the train's horn through his own cheek against the glass. The rainfall slackened to a drizzle and the train was gone.

The bells clanged into silence and the flashing lights quit. The sky lit up again and Bobby noticed the rigid outline of the abandoned laundromat across the street. A light shone in a window on the second floor.

"Who lives there?" he asked.

Frank drooled on his shoulder, moaning in a dream.

"Nobody," he answered himself.

Bobby thought he saw someone stand up in the room above the laundromat and go to the window and wave, but when he wiped the foggy glass inside the phone booth, the vision dissolved into a blurry image seen through the beaded moisture on the glass. He dug into his pocket and retrieved the dime Harry had given him for the phone call. He was to call his mother at the marina and find out what time she would come home. Harry needed to know because he wanted to go to Searchlight with his friend, Emmet Ray. Bobby knew Harry didn't want to watch him and his brother. He dropped the dime into the slot and picked up the phone receiver. Then he dialed the number Harry had given him.

"2-8-9 . . . 2-8-5-4" he repeated each number as he found it on the phone's dial face.

"Hello?" a woman answered.

"Hello," said Bobby. He was not use to talking on phones. He stared hard at the misty glass in front of him, trying to conjure up a picture of the woman.

"This is the Top Rock Marina. Can I help you?"

Bobby paused to think, how could she help him? Why would she want to? Did she already know who he was?

"This is Bobby," he said.

"Hello, Bobby . . . I'm Elaine, now can you tell me what you want. I'm real busy here tonight."

"Is my mama there?"

"What's her name?"

"Mama."

The woman laughed, as if someone were tickling her. "Honey pie, what's your last name. Maybe, if you're lucky, she has the same one."

"Smith. Bobby Smith, My brother is Frank."

He heard her yelling his last name at the marina. She was gone for a few seconds, then came back on the line.

"Sorry, Bobby, but there's no Mother Smiths here tonight," she said. Her voice sounded very far away. "Thanks for calling the Top Rock Marina." She hung up.

The call was over before he knew it. The dime did not come back. Frank pressed against him heavily and his own body was pushed up against the fogged glass. The rain still trickled on the roof, barely a murmur. Bobby traced his finger on the wet pane. The lines appeared bold and clear. He occupied himself for awhile, drawing circles, triangles, letters and numbers. Then he stopped and stared at what he had written, silent and serene. He did not feel the cold anymore.

Harry and Emmet Ray were having another beer. Emmet Ray sat red-faced with pleasure and disgust. Harry just looked worried. The race was still going, the barroom full of the locust buzz of droning engines. A black and white screen was perched on a shelf above bottles of whiskey and vodka and gin. Sharp blades of movement cut across the screen, sending out shadows of lights over the glassy rows of liquor. Each time a car went past the camera a sudden crescendo of noise was swallowed up in speed.

"Get back in there, Unser, you sorry sonuvabitch!" Emmet Ray yelled at the television. "He's been in the pits for five minutes!"

Harry laughed and sipped his beer. "He's probably eatin' some of his mama's world famous chili con carne."

"He can eat all he wants after the goddam race is over! Can't he see Andretti is catching up?" He took his beer and drained it in one long anguishing gulp. The mug came down hard on the counter and Emmet Ray glanced over at the bartender. "Bud," he said, "two more right over here."

Across the bar, a burly man with flaming red hair was pouring beer. He slapped the spigot off as the glass came to a perfect head, just a trace of foam edging over the lip. Emmet Ray and Harry watched him with admiration.

"Nobody does that better than Bud Walker," Emmet Ray beamed.

Harry nodded, "Nobody."

Bud glanced over at them, winked, and retrieved two fresh mugs from under the bar. He was clad in a Hawaiian shirt, unbuttoned halfway down to expose a chest of bristly red hair. He wore a silver watchband imbedded with turquoise, and several rings flashed on his thick fingers. He brought the beers over and took Emmet Ray's money, then paused to observe the race before going to make change.

"How's the picture?" he asked.

"Pretty good, Bud," said Emmet Ray, ". . . better than the VFW ever gets, I'll tell you."

Harry piped in, "Ford's rootin' for Unser and it don't look like he's gonna finish the race."

"That right, Emmet Ray?" Bud mocked curious.

"Yeah."

"Don't you know that what you are lookin' at on the screen took place in Atlanta two hours ago?"

"No, I didn't think . . ."

"No," interrupted Harry, "you sure didn't!"

"Aw, shuddup, Hardy. You never picked a winner in your life. Who are you to talk?"

Bud grinned and shook his head, then walked over to the cash register to ring up the beers.

Harry looked towards the front door. "I wonder where those boys are?"

"What boys?" Emmet Ray stared morosely at the screen.

"Dottie's boys, Bobby and Frank. I sent them over to call Dottie from the pay phone. Let her know we had plans tonight and she would have to be home early."

"What's with that Frank? He some kind of idiot or something?"

"Had a fever when he was a baby. Burned his poor little brain right up. Now, that Bobby is a smart one . . . old for his age, if you know what I mean."

"Kids, you can have 'em."

"I don't want 'em either, but Dottie is a friend and I can't jus' take off and have those two walkin' the streets in the rain."

"Why not? Their mother did."

"Yeah, I suppose she did."

"Earline always wanted kids." Emmet Ray looked down into his beer as if it were a well gone dry. "But I wouldn't hear of it."

"Yeah, well, this ain't no place to raise a family, that's for damn sure."

Bud came back wiping his hands on a towel. "So how is the race coming along, Emmet Ray? Should be just about over. Want me to tell you who won it?"

Emmet Ray shrugged and took another drink of beer. "What I guessed was the Unser brothers were teaming up to get Andretti. Bobby was gonna chase him all afternoon while Al just ran his race the way he wanted to. But it looks like Al's car gave out somewhere around the four-fifty mark, and now Andretti has the field right where he wants it. Bobby can't catch him either."

"A pure and simple shame," Harry teased. "Next time we'll just drive up to Laughlin and play blackjack." Harry nudged his friend with an elbow.

"Be careful, Harry," Emmet Ray snarled. " I ain't in the mood for none of your needling."

"Stick it to him, Harry," Bud whispered loudly. "He deserves it for being such a pigeon."

Harry laughed. "Maybe, that's why Earline left him for that parts salesman." This triggered Emmet Ray, who was drunk, to take a halfhearted swing at his best friend. Missing by several inches, he fell off the stool and landed on his side on the floor. Harry was wheezing with laughter and pointing down at Emmet Ray, who lay there for awhile, mortified.

"Goddam you, Hardy," he fumed, rising to his knees. "Goddam you!"

"Calm down, Ford," said Bud.

"He can't help it," Harry choked back his laughter. "Ever since that clown brained him with a soda bottle, he's been like this."

"Just don't push me." Emmet Ray straightened his shirt and climbed back onto the bar stool. He sat with his beer, looking mournful, and Harry grew silent beside him, nibbling from a bowl of Spanish peanuts. On the screen, race cars whizzed by like insects trapped in a jar.

"I'm about done," said Coyote.

"With what?" Willy wanted to know.

"Sailing," he said.

Willy looked over at him. The rain had left Coyote limp and wasted, like a slightly melted wax figurine. His black hair collapsed across his face, hiding it. Both knees were folded over the gutter. His hands dangled lifelessly from the sleeves of his coat, the pallid color of exposed roots. His head hung down between his legs and his voice had a buried sound to it.

". . . we are sailing on a ship to the Yucatan."

"Sounds like Johnny Earth Tongue's been whisperin' in your ear."

Coyote coughed, a bitter hacking at his lungs.

"We need to get out of this rain, my friend," said Two Childs. "How about my plan to go see Mr. Ford over at BUD'S? He likes to talk and we're good listeners. Maybe, he will buy us a beer or two just for the pleasure of our company."

"I'm awful dry," Coyote admitted.

Willy scoffed. "You keep saying that, but you should see yourself. You look like a drowned muskrat."

Coyote made a motion with his hands, waving them as if the wind had suddenly risen. The gesture seemed to say that he no longer moved or spoke of his own accord, as though his lack of volition was a sign that some larger force had replaced his broken will. The rain was a solemn mist, whispering on the pavement. Into the quiet rushed the swirling flow of water towards the storm drains, where it disappeared on a course of underground culverts to the river, a mile east of town.

Willy finally stood. "Enough of this, Coyote. Get up!"

Coyote managed to raise his head and look up.

"I ain't jokin', let's go get warm. My balls ache in this cold. And you look like a damn ghost."

"A spirit, you mean. A bad omen."

"Please quit with the shaman talk."

"Okay, okay . . . I will cut it out with this knife in my boot."

"You what?"

"Nothing." Coyote Tom struggled to his feet, grabbing Willy by the arm for balance, pulling him close. Willy caught the smell of him and nearly gagged.

"Don't be stupid, Coyote. That knife will land you in jail if you show it to anyone in this bar."

"They left something inside me," Coyote repeated. "Those doctors in Saigon."

The rain ceased. The sky was as black as it had been before the storm broke, but now retained a potent, ominous silence. A purplish light from the town hung suspended in the low cloud cover. Water continued to gurgle along the street, dripping from buildings and lamp posts and parked cars. The wind carried strong wisps of greasewood and creosote, pushed in from the desert. The smell seemed to brace Coyote, as he shook water from his shoulders and back. The two Indians moved together as one towards the entrance to BUD'S (Beer and Wine).

The radio signal grew stronger once Pomona drove away from the overpass. The preacher was finishing off a long list of current events that had been predicted in the Bible, and now he was describing the Judgment Day which was scheduled to arrive sometime before the close of the century. This was Pomona's favorite part of the program and he turned the volume knob as loud as it would go over the cylindrical chatter of the pickup's engine.

". . . before God Almighty we will all stand, each individual absolved of humanity, each man or woman alone before the Lord with his acts and deeds. There can be no mystery to the trial's outcome. All evidence stands revealed. Brethren, know in your hearts that the end is near. Reading from Acts 2:17 . . . 'And in the last days it shall be, God declares, that I will pour out my Spirit upon all flesh, and your sons shall have prophesies and your young men shall see visions, and your old men shall dream dreams . . . And I will show wonders in the heaven above and signs on the earth below, blood, and fire, and vapor of smoke . . . the sun shall be turned into darkness and the

moon into blood, before the day of the Lord comes, the
great and manifest day. And it shall be that whoever calls
on the name of the Lord shall be saved.' Think of that,
brethren. 'And it shall be that whoever calls on the name of
the LOOOORRRRD shall be saved' . . . Feels good,
brothers and sisters, it surely does . . . LOOOOOOOR-
RRRRRRRD . . . Say      it      with      me      now . . .
JEEEEEEEEESUS . . . What's wrong with that?"

He turned it down but not off as he approached town.
In his rearview mirror, the bridge appeared as nothing
more than a string of blue lights across the river gorge.
Then he noticed several headlights parked out on the
bridgespan and looked back over his shoulder. He wondered what was going on back there. It seemed strange to
see them all stopped together like that. Pomona wondered if there could have been an accident on the bridge,
one bad enough to stop traffic. It wasn't likely. He
decided not to turn around and find out. He had already
logged two hours of overtime getting the last of the palms
in the ground. He just wanted to drink a beer or two
among friends and go home to bed.

The frontage road ran along the Interstate for about a
mile before it veered off in the direction of the river. He
began to pass empty buildings, the cinderblock shells of
deserted stores and service stations which were still operating a year ago, before the completion of the new Interstate business loop. Not another car was on the road with
him tonight.

He finally came to the edge of town. The first streets
were cinder tracks running through an unlit neighborhood of adobe shacks and trailer homes, dead-ending
with their gravel tails swallowed back by the desert. This
was where the migrant farmworkers lived, the ones who
stacked crates or picked lettuce for a season and left.
Then came the paved streets, wide curbed lanes named
for New World explorers like Drake, Magellan, and

De Gama. He turned left on Main and drove slowly down the wet street.

Since the rain had stopped, everything looked washed and shiny and clean, even the brick facade of the abandoned laundromat. The bars started about half way down the block. He slowed as he passed each one, trying to see through a jarred door or an unfogged window, but he could tell nothing about what was going on inside. He didn't need to; he already knew what he would find.

After they saw the Indians enter the bar where Harry was, the brothers stepped out of the phone booth into the rinsed air. They walked along the sidewalk, bundled together and moving as one four-legged animal through the blinking neon towards a three-story building at the end of the block. Bobby held fast to Frank and stared ahead at the courthouse, rising clear and white above the crabgrass lawn which circled it like a moat. Bobby knew the courthouse was empty. Harry had told him how the judges used to arrive by steamboat, in the days of the mining camps, to sentence renegades and outlaws to life terms in the territorial prison at Yuma. Nobody came to the courthouse nowadays. It sat useless beside the boarded-up post office and abandoned laundromat, old and hollow and haunted.

When they reached the end of the block, they climbed the white stone steps. Bobby tugged Frank's arm and they stopped to rest on the top slab. From here they had a view of the block of bars in downtown Solero. They could look west towards the desert or east towards the river, but it was too dark now to tell the difference. They sat close together, trying to stay warm.

"We ain't going back in there," said Bobby. "We'll just wait for Harry to come out."

Frank closed his eyes, leaning closer to his brother for safety. His bland face became restful and serene.

"We'll just wait right here 'til he comes out, and then we can go to his house to meet mama. At midnight."

Bobby turned slightly to look over his shoulder at the courthouse. What he saw for an instant was the building ablaze with light, then a crack of thunder stepped down from the sky. He imagined smoke pouring from seams in the boarded windows, orange flames dancing on the roof of the old post office, and the blackest smoke of all issuing in thick streams from the garret window above the abandoned laundromat. Rain dripped from the high cornices of the courthouse, clapping into puddles on the cracked flagstone porch. The vision he had seen was gone now and the other buildings rested silently beyond the courthouse. The cowboy's shadow moved away from the garret window and the lamplight above the laundromat winked out.

He sat rigidly up and glanced down the street.

"Somebody's comin'!" he whispered. Farther down the street, the lights of a pickup were searching for them slowly. He took his brother by the coat sleeves and yanked him awake again. The truck had slowed to a crawl, still half the distance of the block away. They watched the Highway Department vehicle inch along the street, stopping for a moment before one bar, then moving on to the next. Frank began to gurgle and Bobby had to rub his hands to calm him. A purple vein of lightning flashed down into the blackness west of town and the rumbling sky erupted in thunder. The boys jumped involuntarily, then cowered down in their cold seats on the courthouse steps. The truck pulled up under the red and blue lights of BUD'S (Beer and Wine) and stopped. The engine puttered out. A man in a dark green poncho sat inside. Bobby could see him sitting there, smoking a cigarette. He thought he could hear a radio playing somewhere nearby.

The wind dragged across her face and hair like a rough comb, but Dottie's chest and legs were protected, and her hands stayed warm wrapped around Chain's beltline. The road aimed east at a gradual incline, lit by the piercing headlamps of a dozen racing machines. The sound of all the engines running together was tremendous, and Dottie felt herself in the midst of a surging wave of power, advancing over the glassy highway with a tidal force. There were bikes in front of and beside and behind her, as if she were something precious enough to be surrounded and protected from others who might try to take it away. Holding tight to a man she feared, she didn't permit herself to consider how dangerous the situation might be.

"How does it feel?" Chain yelled.

"I don't know," she leaned her face up against the back of his neck to speak.

"You don't know," he called out, "'cause you never felt anything like it before."

He was right. She had been on a motorcycle before, but it was a little dirt bike, nothing like this. This was something else, like riding on the back of an extremely wild animal, completely harnessed to her fate.

"It's fine, I guess." When she said this her mouth touched his ear and he swiveled around to kiss her. She felt the bike swoop as he changed the balance of weight. A picture of the trailer where she lived came into her mind, cramped and dirty, with her boys' bed still unmade and unwashed dishes piled on the tiny cutting board. And she thought of an ex-husband, his face a blur, coming after her one night to give her a beating for going out without him. Which bar or which town or even which husband, she couldn't be sure, but it was a scene that had played itself out in one sad way or another for as long as she had been married. Twenty years, at least. One thing gave her comfort and that was the conviction that nobody was coming after her tonight. She tightened her grip around Chain's waist. Dottie didn't know what she was doing, or how the night would end, but all at once the feelings of heat and speed and unalterable direction seemed like a fair alternative to another night in Solero.

"Don't kiss me!" she screamed. "Just keep this thing on the highway!"

"Geezus H. Christ!" groaned Emmet Ray. "Ain't it a bitch?"

"That it is," Harry nodded. He was trying to be agreeable and keep an eye on his buddy. Emmet Ray was not himself, he could see, and it was his duty to keep him out of trouble. "That it surely is."

"Why'd she have to go and leave me? Didn't I work hard enough to keep her happy? I built that business up from scratch, goddamit! Is it my fault they built the goddam freeway on the other side of town?"

"Coffee, Bud," said Harry, "two of them. Black."

Bud nodded, wiping down the bar where Emmet Ray had spilled some beer. He was shaking his head and looking at Harry, chiding him with a sideways smile. He brought a stool out from under the bar and, standing on it, turned the television off. Harry noticed that the bar had emptied, and they were the only customers. He thought about Dottie's boys, but he was presently more worried about Emmet Ray's morose condition.

"Not much of a race, was it?" Bud said.

"Nope," said Emmet Ray. "How about a beer?"

Harry looked at Bud again. "Let's switch to coffee, Emmet Ray. We want to be fresh for the drive to Bullhead City, don't we?"

"You drink mine for me. You'll be twice as fresh."

"Look," said Harry, "I'm sorry I made that crack about Earline. I guess I misjudged your mood or somethin'. Anyways, I didn't mean it. You know that."

"Shut up, Harry. Will you do that much for me? Just shut up, okay?"

Harry patted Emmet Ray on the back. "You ain't thinkin' about knockin' me off this stool again, are ya?"

Emmet Ray brushed Harry's hand away. "Lay off me, Harry . . . I swear to God . . . just lay off." He took a last draining swig of his beer, then let the mug come down hard on the counter. He stared up at the blank television screen above the bar. The liquor bottles glinted and shined, reflecting the changing colors in the window. From the back of the room came the humming of a heater just starting up.

Bud came back with the coffees and set one down in front of each of them. Harry took his cheerfully and sipped it. Emmet Ray remained morose, gazing at the television. He still gripped his empty beer mug with both hands. Bud wiped a series of rings from the opposite end of the bar. The bright red cloth flicked on the bartop as he worked towards them with quick furious movements of his wrist.

Coyote Tom blundered into the room ahead of Mr. Willy Two Childs. He tripped twice over chairs, swaying as he rose. He set his hands flat on one of the tables and steadied himself. He looked up at the three staring white faces.

"Two good soldiers," he grunted.

Willy took hold of Coyote by the shoulder, following close behind. "Sorry, Mr. Ford. My friend is drunk."

"Don't worry," said Harry, "he don't need no excuse to fall down around here."

"What do you bucks want?" Bud demanded. His voice echoed loudly in the empty barroom.

"We want to talk to Mr. Ford about a job." Willy had folded Coyote into a chair and stepped forward to address the three white men.

"Job?" said Emmet Ray, "You mean you need a tow? Tonight? Sorry, fella, but I ain't open right now. Probably drunker than your friend there, if the truth be known."

"We want to make you a deal," Willy persisted.

"Why don't you two turn around and go back where you came from," Bud said. "I don't need any damn Indians botherin' what few customers I got left."

"You don't understand. We want to work for Mr. Ford, here."

"Work," Emmet Ray coughed, "for me?"

Willy nodded, smiling. "We always noticed how you have trouble stayin' open after dark. We figured you just couldn't find nobody willin' to sit out there in that station, waitin' for them tourists to drive through in the middle of night. Well, we might be able to help."

"Might be able to help?" said Emmet Ray. He looked at Harry and Bud and smirked. "These two might be able to help."

Bud was getting impatient with the whole conversation. His hands disappeared below the counter. "Why don't you two get out of here before I get mad." Emmet Ray and Harry both looked at Bud. His pink face was growing crimson and the hair on his chest seemed to flame out over the vee of his tropical shirt.

"What if we buy drinks?" asked Willy, glancing over his shoulder at the slumped figure of Coyote Tom.

"Let me see your money, then I'll show you my liquor." Bud's hands remained out of sight below the bartop. They moved mysteriously and a metallic click sounded. Emmet Ray and Harry exchanged wary glances and looked back towards the two Indians at the table across the room.

"We can pay," Willy insisted.

"With what?" replied Bud.

"We have a coin, worth hundreds, a gold piece from the Spaniard's treasure."

"Yeah? Let's see it."

"We don't want to sell it. We only want to use it for a loan. We both have day jobs and can pay you back next Friday night, with interest."

"I haven't seen any coin yet," said Bud.

"My friend has it right here." Willy motioned towards Coyote Tom. The pouch hung from a leather string around his neck. Willy reached for it, but Coyote stood up and pushed him away.

"No," said Coyote. "No more."

"These men want to see it is all," Willy pointed at Harry and Emmet Ray.

"Who are they?" Coyote asked, using his hands on the table to support himself. "Viet Cong?"

"Maybe we oughta call the Sheriff, Bud." Harry didn't like the way things were developing in the room. He hoped the boys wouldn't come back anytime soon.

"I don't think so," Bud growled. Both Harry and Emmet Ray could see he was getting angry. They didn't like that, either.

Emmet Ray turned to Bud and whispered, "What do you want us to do, throw 'em out?" Bud said nothing. His hands remained below the counter. Then he set a small pistol on the bar and covered it with the red towel.

When Harry looked back at the Indians, they were wrestling on the table. Willy had grabbed at the pouch and Coyote pulled him down by the arm. They struggled briefly and then Willy managed to subdue the weakened Coyote, holding him by the neck down upon the table. Coyote's chin rested over the edge and he snorted like an animal trying hard to breath. Willy's back was to them, so he didn't see the gun, and Coyote's face was lost in a black tangle of hair.

"Listen to me, Coyote, we will get the coin back. We can hock it tonight and buy it back next Friday."

Coyote grunted, but did not resist. Willy had his knee firmly planted in the small of Coyote's back. He leaned over Coyote, untied the pouch and loosened it from around his neck. He emptied the pouch, a single feather bobbing from its leather fringe, and the coin bounced on the table alongside Coyote's head.

"Is it real gold?" asked Emmet Ray.

"Yes, given to my friend by his grandfather who took it from a cave in the mountains south of Top Rock."

"The Spaniard's treasure, you say?" Harry was doubtful.

Bud said nothing, wiping his hands nervously on the red towel. Emmet Ray and Harry watched him with brief uncertain glances. A tension had fallen over the room. It seemed to travel through the air, electric and volatile, as if charged by the storm outside. Bud's bright blue eyes were riveted on the table where the coin lay beside the two Indians. Willy had eased his grip on Coyote, but he kept his knee burrowed into the spine of his friend. The coin rested to one side of Coyote's pinned shoulders, near the table's edge.

"We will have enough whiskey to warm us through the night," Willy spoke to Coyote in a soothing croon, "and enough left over for your cousin, too."

Coyote made a muffled noise in his throat, as if he were choking on a piece of meat.

". . . or we can take the money and go up to the pink motel in Searchlight. Buy us a real nice time with two of Rosie's girls . . . Wouldn't that be a fine way to ride out this storm?"

"No more!" Coyote yelled.

"What do you aim to do, Bud?" Harry asked.

"Let's boot them outta here," said Emmet Ray, rolling up his sleeves. His eyes were fixed on the coin.

Bud did not answer, studying the tableau before him; two soaked Indians struggling upon one of his tables. He watched Willy release his grip and reach for the coin. The gold piece gave a quick yellow flash and disappeared into his bony fingers. Willy got off Coyote and turned to the bar, waving his hand in the air victoriously. Coyote did not stir.

"I have it," he said.

"Bring it here," said Bud. He placed both hands on the counter, the red towel between them over the gun. Willy looked down again at Coyote's motionless body, then stepped towards the bar.

"Look out!" cried Harry.

Coyote had sprung awake, tackling Willy from behind, sending both of them sprawling. As they tumbled toward the bar, Emmet Ray gave a swift kick which glanced off Coyote's head. Then Willy had Emmet Ray by the ankle and the stool came out from under him. Emmet Ray hit the ground screaming. Willy and Coyote wrestled beside him and the coin rolled away from them. Emmet Ray scrambled to pick it up. Coyote lunged at him, but Willy held him back. The two Indians rolled across the floor, banging into table legs and sending chairs flying. Emmet Ray stood up breathing heavily, the goldpiece in his hand.

"Don't!" Willy groaned. "Give it to me."

"Yes!" Coyote bellowed, his black hair wrapped around his face.

"Give it to me," Willy grunted again, "before you get us busted. There. I have it."

Coyote finally collapsed in a pile of twisted arms and bent legs. Willy stood up, the knife glinting silver in his upheld hand.

"I have it," he repeated.

The sound of a gunshot cracked against the walls, as Emmet Ray and Harry looked on in horror. It cracked again and the room went silent. Bud put the pistol down on top of the bar, and resumed wiping the counter with his rag.

As though suddenly released from some intolerable suspension, the rain poured down again. The street corner was bathed in a flowing light, first green, then yellow, then red. The two shots had come like distant thunder cracks, yet without the long cavernous rumblings, as if they had been cut short, swallowed up in mid-note. The two boys huddled in the doorway of the courthouse, unsure of what to do or where to go. Bobby stared at the Highway Department pickup and at the dark silhouette inside. The rain came down harder and harder, sweeping over the street and curb with a vicious hissing. Instantly, the gutters were flooding up over the sidewalks as great pools of water formed over the clogged stormdrains. Then the door of the pickup swung open and a man climbed out. He pulled up his collar under his hat and moved swiftly towards the door of BUD'S (Beer and Wine). Bobby watched the glass door shine as he pulled it open, flashing again as it swung shut. And then, as suddenly as it had started, the cloudburst ceased. A few swift sparse drops fell on the stone steps of the courthouse and the quiet returned.

Bobby seized Frank's hand and tugged him out from the cover of the doorway. They ran down the steps and across the street. Still afraid to go inside, they paced back and forth in front of the bar window. The blinds were half-cracked and the alternating neon shone red, white and blue, but Bobby could not see Harry or anything else in there. He pulled at Frank's shoulder and pointed down the street, in the direction of the railroad tracks.

"Come on, Frank," he said. "They've killed Harry. Those Indians did. We have to go find mama and tell her about it."

They took off at a trot, passing each bar and store before leaving the burning lights of town and entering the darkness which surrounded Solero like a circular wall. They came to the tracks, Frank stumbling up the cinders behind his younger brother. He cried and showed Bobby his hands.

"You bleeding, Frank?"

Frank sniffled and sobbed. He had landed on the tracks with his hands outstretched and now they were scraped and bloody. He felt frightened and tired and he didn't understand why they had to leave the town behind. He looked at Bobby pleadingly, hoping to be taken home.

"We got to find mama. She's over there."

Bobby was pointing into the desert to the east. A river was out there somewhere, he knew, and a bridge. The railroad crossed the bridge into Arizona. The marina dance was in Arizona, just across that span of highway. They could make it in an hour if they hurried, maybe less. Stepping on the oily crossties that ran beneath the slick silver rails, Bobby took his brother's injured hand and led him away.

"Christ almighty!" Emmet Ray gasped. "What the hell did you do, Bud?"

The room reeked with a stong burning smell and a grey vapor still floated over the bar. Bud did not answer Emmet Ray. He was busy wiping the .38 clean with the red towel, looking down now and then at the two bodies slumped together on the barroom floor. He finally put the pistol back under the counter and shrugged.

"Nothing," he said quietly.

"Nothing?" said Harry. "Nothing? My lord, Bud . . . you just shot two men."

Bud looked blankly at Harry. "Two drunk Indians, you mean."

"I know that, Bud, but, hell . . . you can't shoot Indians just because they're drunk."

"Two drunk Indians waving a knife at my customers."

"Oh," Harry said, "is that it? Is that your story? Now we're in this thing, too? Is that it?"

Bud said nothing. The room was silent save for the tick of the heater at the back, near the rear exit.

"We gotta do somethin', Bud," Emmet Ray was kneeling over the bodies, but unwilling to touch them. He stood up and walked back to the bar, picking up his bar stool in the process. "This could mean big trouble for you."

"This ain't nothin'," Bud sneered, "unless you two try to make it somethin'."

"Now, look, Bud," Harry said. "We sat here and saw the whole thing. You can't try to buffalo us into . . ."

"You never heard of self-defense?"

"This wasn't . . ."

"It was a judgment call, Harry! I judged those two to be a threat to me, my customers and my property. How was I to know whether that bastard with the knife wasn't going to lean over and cut your throat?"

"He was takin' the knife away from the other one, Bud. You saw that. We all saw that."

Emmet Ray shook his head. "I dunno, Harry. Maybe Bud is right."

"Hell yes, I'm right," Bud said. "Not a jury in this county that would see it any other way."

They all turned at the sound of the front door. It swung open and before they could move he walked in. Jose Pomona stopped just inside the room, removing his dripping hat and unbuttoning his rain-soaked poncho. He stopped when he saw the bodies.

"Hey, Joey boy," said Bud. "Come on in."

Emmet Ray sat down on his stool and Harry shifted uncomfortably to look at Pomona. They both looked back and eyed Bud with distrust, but his hands remained calm and in the open. "Step up here and let me get you a cold one."

Pomona continued unbuttoning his poncho, but he did not move towards them. Neither did he back away. His expression was one of mild curiosity, as if someone had just told a joke which he had only heard the last part of.

"You're just the man I wanted to see." Bud came out from behind the bar with his keys. He walked over to Pomona, patted him on the shoulder and went to lock the front door. Then he hurried over and closed the blinds, put the closed sign in the window and set the deadbolt on the back exit.

"You seem kind of nervous tonight, Bud." This was Pomona talking. He hung his hat and poncho on a peg by the door and came across the room, staying clear of the bodies. "Anything wrong?"

Bud came back behind the bar after checking the street through the window. He walked around the bodies, avoiding the red pool which had spread across the floor between them. Pomona had taken a seat a safe distance from the others, at the far end of the bar near the register. He looked from the Indians to Emmet Ray and Harry to Bud, and then back to the Indians, like it was a picture he couldn't quite get in focus.

"So," he said, breaking a long silence, "are those men drunk or dead?"

"Bud shot 'em," said Harry.

"Why?"

"Simple," answered Bud. "These two crazies came in here wavin' a knife and demandin' liquor. I felt my life was in danger so I let 'em have it. Simple as that."

Pomona nodded, "That's simple, alright."

Bud put his hands below the counter and aimed his chin at Emmet Ray and Harry. "Just ask them if that ain't what happened."

"Yeah," Emmet Ray piped in, "exactly like Bud said. You can see the knife over there on the floor."

"Did they know you had a gun?" asked Pomona.

"How should I know?" Bud said. "It ain't a secret I try to keep from anybody, if that's what you're drivin' at."

"What I'm drivin' at is, it sounds like suicide for those
two to come in here with that little buck knife and try to
cut you down holdin' a loaded gun."

"I can't say what was on their minds, now can I, Joey?
Indians are hard to figure, sometimes."

Pomona didn't say anything for awhile. Bud poured him
a beer and he drank it down. Then he had another. Harry
and Emmet Ray sat drinking cold coffee, both afraid of
what Bud might do if they crossed him. Bud brought out a
pail and a mop and worked on the blood for awhile, then
thought better of it and came back behind the bar. When
Pomona was done with the second beer, he spoke again.

"Well now, Bud, what are you planning to do?"

"I been thinking that over," said Bud. "I honestly have."

"Yeah, I imagine you have."

"And what I been thinking is this. If I call the Sheriff and
he comes over here and takes down my statement and
interviews these two fools and goes home to make his
report, then everyone in this room will spend time in the
Riverside court. I ain't denyin' I killed them two drunks.
And a jury gets picked and the lawyers fight it out and I
have to drive to the county seat every week for the trial. It
could take a month or two, how would I know. And God
knows what it would end up costin' me, not to mention the
taxpayers."

"No. Let's not forget the taxpayers," Pomona added.

"It just seems like a waste, 'cause there ain't a jury in hell
is gonna convict me of murder in a case like this. I was
defendin' my property and my customers and I have the
witnesses to prove it."

Pomona looked hard at Harry and Emmet Ray, remaining close-mouthed on their respective bar stools.

"So . . . you still haven't answered my question."

"No?"

"What are you planning to do?"

Bud smiled. "You want another beer, Joey?"

"Not just yet."

"Okay, okay," said Bud, wiping the bartop clean with mindless circlings of the red towel. "Here it is . . . my plan. I find someone with a truck and a shovel, someone I can trust to keep his mouth shut and his eyes open, if you know what I mean." He glared at Harry, then went on. "And if I could find someone like that, I would be willin' to pay a price to get those two Indians underground before the sun comes up tomorrow. Then I find their vehicle and drive it up the road a couple of miles and plunge it off a cliff into the river."

Emmet Ray and Harry looked at Pomona. They both knew who Bud was talking about, and they figured he did too. But Pomona just sat there, fingering his empty mug and staring down into the suds at the bottom of it.

"You'd be doin' me a big favor, Joey," Bud whispered.

"I'd be risking my ass," he answered.

"I'd make it worth your while."

"Oh?"

"You'd have to work a month of Sundays to get what I'd pay you for a couple hours of diggin' tonight."

Pomona shrugged. Bud grinned, then turned to the others.

"Wrap those two up in tablecloths and drag them over to the back door. I'll bring Joe's truck around myself."

Harry and Emmet Ray both hesitated, looking to Pomona for some sign or gesture of agreement. Then Bud reached under the counter and they jumped down off their stools, hurrying to cover the bodies in cheap vinyl cloth.

"I can't tell you what this means to me, Joey boy."

Pomona looked up at Bud.

"I haven't agreed to anything yet," he said.

"No?" Bud smiled. "You haven't."

"What is the going rate for risking an accessory-to-murder charge?"

"Well, hold out your hand a second."

Bud dropped the coin into Pomona's dirty, outstretched palm.

*R*arely did anyone bother turning back to examine the feeble heart of Solero. A bumpy frontage road curled down alongside the rockstrewn gully, which had been a branch of the river before the complex system of dikes and aqueducts upriver siphoned off the water and reduced it to a flaked gravel wash. At the end of this road, the original railroad town sizzled beside the dry riverbed in the withering heat, a nostalgic collection of wooden false fronts, corrugated tin buildings and brick-and-adobe bars. The courthouse, jail and post office were boarded up and the laundromat was abandoned. Old Solero sat forgotten, connected to the rest of the world by only a frontage road marred with potholes, sand drifts and lumps of volcanic cinder.

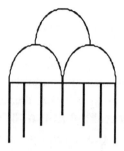

# The Elsinore Cowboy's Good-bye

The Elsinore Cowboy said goodbye in April, a month no crueler than any other, but with a remarkable talent for sudden winds which loosened the phone poles and misdirected the road signs and rearranged the trailer parks from Twenty-nine Palms clear to Kingman, arriving with the unequalled fury of a Biblical cyclone and defeating the purpose not only of the buzzards and crows and hawks but even of the golden eagles who were forced into high aeries to wait out the storm in the carrion stench of previous kills, perched erect and somnolent until May floated in with its bright oppressive heat which paralyzed the lizards in the cracks of the sidewalks and pinned down the diamondbacks in the red shade of fallen billboards as the paint cracked and peeled in bright chips from the transoms and doorways of the shops and houses of Solero, whose entire population yawned in dull anticipation, the awful thought of the coming summer numbing all their hearts, the specter of that fearsome season melting all their illusions, the mere mention of that flammable noun

igniting all their sorrow, as the railyard workers moaned
and the gas pump attendants whimpered and the coffee
shop waitresses wept openly in front of their customers,
while the Indians got drunk and the divorced real estate
agents got drunker and the auto mechanics got drunkest
of all so that anybody who broke down in late spring was
stuck there until October when the terrible lethargy
finally began to subside, and, worse than that, the
prostitutes from Searchlight all took temporary jobs in
Las Vegas to replace the regular girls who vacationed on
the coast, and although they were just as ugly as ever they
cost twice as much now because no matter what
unforgiving hand the heat might deal a gambler would be
there to play it and the North Vegas cat houses were done
up in cheap imitations of late night television westerns in
which the dirt-caked, dung-smudged outlaw spends his
last silver dollar in the velvet-draped parlor as the troops
of fledgling actresses fight for a seat in the leading man's
lap and the horses whinny and the sun goes down the
color of someone else's blood, because what dollar-
minded film director in his right mind would have the
hero die in bed with his boots off, not even Sam
Peckinpah, when the winds began to lift and the
lobster-colored hands could be seen in the windowsill of
the second story garret above the abandoned laundromat
on Main Street, which the people of Solero had suspected
all along was a hotel for inveterate vagabaonds deposited
into the nearby railyards by slow-moving freight cars
from Winslow, Red Bluff or Tucumcari, because although
they knew the doors were locked and the windows were
boarded up with plywood left over from all the new
construction along the Interstate business loop west of
town, the dim signs of life kept brushing at the garret
curtains and a slow accumulation of waste had built up in
the alley behind the dilapidated structure that nobody
could remember who owned, just as nobody had seen the

occupant's real face which was a mask of pain he kept in a
Stetson hatbox on the nightstand beside the wheelchair of
his misfortunes, and the asthmatic dentists vacationed
and the railroad officers retired and the Highway
Department head supervisor was transferred to a better
climate, leaving only Jack Nooncaster and his truculent
roadcrews to maintain order, and the beauticians left
town and the farmworkers went on strike and the AWOL
Marines stole cars and fled to Los Angeles, so all that
remained of the original town was a main artery of empty
bars and closed businesses, a few blocks of blistered
housing, and an occasional coyote wandering through the
railyard cinders, while the last human inhabitants curled
up next to their air conditioners and read each book from
Genesis to Revelations aloud to combat the stifling
silence.

Had it been September he might have tried to hold on,
but springtime in the desert was only a careless match
tossed towards the vacant lot of August, with a slow wick
that burned the days away fifteen hours at a time,
accompanied by the sounds of desperate ground rodents
dying in coils of shedding snakeskin, and the mosquitoes
plotting like a conspiracy of anarchists in the brackish
pools left by the receding river in the alluvial delta north
of Top Rock, and the scorpions brewing their venom in
the darkened laboratories of the earth, not to mention the
alarming disappearance of entire herds of bighorn sheep
contaminated by nuclear fallout during the Nevada tests
of the early 1950's, whose bones apparently disintegrated
from within and evaporated into small clouds of
radioactive dust so that no one could be sure if it was
really safe to breath any longer, causing even more people
to leave the area as Interstate traffic took alternate routes
until the federal government published official reports
denying the existence of the microscopic dust and the ban
on outdoor breathing was lifted just in time for the yearly

convention of the Solero Junk Dealers Association, at which time it was wisely decided that a special fundraising event was necessary in order to draw tourists and their business back to that godforsaken corner of nowhere, a grand spectacle to be advertised as the First Annual Colorado River Bridge Collapse, sponsored jointly by the Highway Department and the SJDA, being a profitable arrangement for both interests, since it enabled Nooncaster to demand construction funds from state monies on both sides of the river and assured his men overtime wages through mid-summer designing and building and destroying the bridge themselves, relying solely on the local junkyards for all the materials needed to construct a scrap metal replica of the London Bridge across the narrowest channel of the swamp (materials which were available at bargain basement rates from early April through late September when all the mechanics were too drunk to walk and every broken down car, truck, bus or motorcycle was left to the brutal garage of the sun) and out of their own generous pockets the dealers supplied the rusted vehicles that were placed on the completed bridge for realistic effect, the time and place of the gala event posted on billboards that the Highway Department rented in both states and as far away as Bellingham, Washington and Bangor, Maine so that on that dreadful Fourth of July morning the town was momentarily revived as the motels filled up and the all-night restaurants actually stayed open all night and the bus station was repainted a glowing shade of blue so that it resembled a huge ice cube dripping on the corner of Magellan and Main while the crowds kept arriving from Spokane and Akron and Pierre with the kids and the dogs and the ice cream melting into the textured carpets of station wagons, everyone standing around the only pool in town telling each other how someone else had said it was supposed to be better than Busch Gardens or the Space

Needle or Six Flags, advertisement mythologies that were
quickly dispelled when on that appointed day they all
drove out to Top Rock swamp with a picnic lunch of beer
and coldcuts and were dismayed to learn that the bridge
being collapsed was neither the legendary Route 66 nor
the fabled Santa Fe line, but only a cheap steel facsimile of
Jack the Ripper fame with welded steel blocks instead of
handcarved granite sustaining a single lane of gummified
asphalt into which the donated cars and pickups had sunk
down to their axles, making them appear more like a
careless child's misplaced toys than the abandoned
vehicles of delirious adults, and the same overweight
Highway Department official who had ever so proudly
announced the completion of the bridge one week earlier
as a great link between two brotherly states now just as
proudly proclaimed its destruction as a living symbol of
our everlasting geographical bond, blah-dee-blah-dee-
blah, while the sun crept higher into the sweatstained sky
and housewives from Indiana fainted and senior citizens
from New Hampshire suffered heat stroke and the whole
crowd was thrown into such a deep personal turmoil by
the time his speech was over that the ensuing explosion
was an insignificant flash in the pocket cameras of their
collective memory, and even the most alert of those
present could not tell if the collapse had actually occurred
or if the whole thing had been induced through solar
hypnosis.

April was a prelude to the fierce high whistle of the
trains arriving at the station down the street, stopping for
precious water while the passengers suffocated in the
almost motionless quality of time as the interminable
unloading of cinderblocks and rebar went on with the
muscular efforts of underpaid Indians in the shadeless
noon heat, work that continued with the same timeless
rhythms as the boxing and stacking and lifting of crates of
lettuce and tomatoes and cauliflower in the irrigated

fields upriver while the farmworkers bent in
brownskinned clusters among the shimmering rows of
green, the heat rising in waves from the ground to drown
them from sight, while the one hundred degree swelter of
his garret above the laundromat became like an oven
which he stared out of and it grew so hot that he thought
he could feel his own intestines roasting against his ribs as
he watched the trains come and go, wincing with the
painful reminder of yet another year alive and alone, the
rodeo calendar in the tiny kitchenette dusty with neglect,
the clock on the dresser broken, his wristwatch unwound,
as if he had decided finally to ignore the relentless beating
of their wings as the angels approached, and his sadness
was intolerable for the tapping had the same stacatto clop
of horse hooves and the days of his youth in Elsinore
galloped across his heart, impaling in it the permanent
drumbeat of nostalgia and his father, too, stood next to
him and wept, muttering over and over that the roosters
must be silenced and the pigs slaughtered and the cows
sold for such were the mutterings of southern California
ranchers in the drought years, and from his chair near the
dirty window above Main Street he could still see the
bloated figures of dead cattle lying in dried out
streambeds and sand-bottomed waterholes, although
anyone else would only have seen the rusting hulks of
abandoned automobiles and the occasional stray coyote
that wandered back and forth through the fugitive streets
like an explorer lost in some unmapped region, yipping
and howling under the old man's window every moonless
night in March, so that in April, along with his aching
nostalgia for a past of musty feed sheds and cavernous
barns came the fantastic and unbridled fear of dogs,
which everyone knows are the real harbingers of
mortality, and when that chorus of howls went up in the
noonday chill of his shooting star nightmare of death in all
its stellar calamity he would kneel down in solemn prayer

to a God he believed in but did not expect to ever see until
the sharp staccato hoofbeats of His messengers could be
heard approaching with increasing speed, mixed
imperceptibly with the hammer cracks of workmen
frantically assembling the foundation of this year's bridge
before the pitiless summer had a chance to wake and
villify the days with the hot smell of its scorching breath,
and so it was then, in April, that he decided to say good-
bye once and for all to that life of erased memories and
forgotten acts since the entire story of his childhood, his
heroic youth, and his crippled old age was the only
currency he had left to pay the landlord of his too, too
long life.

He made a cup of coffee which was weak and sweet as
he preferred it and he sipped lightly while it cooled,
mulling in his head the correct thing to say, the proper
words to use, which would be his anonymous farewell to
the town and to the desert and to the mountains in the
south stabbing at the skyline like rusted knife blades and
to the river in the east ploughing from dam to dam in its
long path of prehistory winding through the rocky
corridors of Top Rock Gorge like a worm down the spine
of some ancient fish embedded in the sedimentary ocean
of the Mojave, and then as the hot brown liquid kissed his
weathered lip of tears— the Elsinore Cowboy—whose
boots were worn, whose clothes were old, whose name
was unknown, whose age was uncertain, whose faith was
weak, whose game was lonely, whose occupation was
wishing, whose patience was unrewarded, whose shade
was twilight, whose tired blood was a miracle of geology,
whose faded voice was the scratching of stones, whose
wrinkled skin was the color of windblown sand, whose
pale eyes were grayer than rain, whose submerged heart
was more porous than a coral beneath the oceanic bedlam
in his soul — the Elsinore Cowboy —whose only desire
was one more moment of public consequence before he

died, gave a deep sigh of discontent and slumped forward
to embrace the sudden April gale that swept in through
the taped glass as he dropped the single electric lamp into
the metal washtub that was still half-full of brackish
mosquito larvae and mildewed eating utensils, all power
on the block shutting abruptly off as that unnoticed
legend of dry bones collapsed to the floor and the lamp
shot green sparks of diffusing energy into the fetid air of
his death throes which were violent and quick.

All hell broke loose in that infamous month of well-bred
disasters as the faulty wiring of the abandoned
laundromat sang with electricity and ignited, the flames
leaping one hundred feet over the ashbeds of the
courthouse and post office and barber shop which were
all instant victims of the fire's instinctive thirst for dried
out beams and walls and porches, an entire block reduced
to cinder along with the laundromat as the rampant
powerlines surged backwards to their source, the town
generator, which exploded, sending shock waves across
the street to the railyard where trains derailed and tracks
switched and signals failed while the strange dominoes of
destruction kept tumbling, the heat from the fire lighting
a natural gas line that led out of town towards the river
where it connected with several others in a white mire of
tubes and tanks which needless to say exploded beside the
nearly completed bridge, collapsing with it a dump truck,
a tractor, a crane, and a ten-man crew from the Highway
Department, so that when people looked out their
windows on that inescapable day in April each one
thought privately that it was time to leave, not so much
because of the black column of smoke rising from the
town square, nor the sirens of the ambulance units rushing
out to Top Rock, nor even the notion that another
inevitable summer was already on its way, but because of
the pervasive echo of his final goodbye which seemed to
haunt the burning air.

DIRK HARMAN was born in Twentynine Palms, California in 1956. He received his B.A. from UC San Diego where he studied anthropology, art and literature. He is a husband, father, teacher and artist as well as a part-time resident of Topock, Arizona where he is at work on another book.